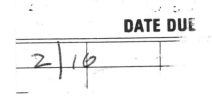

DATE DUE

2/16

HARVEST MOON

A Wisconsin Outdoor Anthology

Edited by Ted Rulseh

Lost River Press
P.O. Box 1381
Woodruff, WI 54568

A Wisconsin Outdoor Anthology

It is a time, this harvest moon, when those who love the land
Come together and celebrate the gifts Earth has bequeathed them.
And to remember their lives are ephemeral, as the fruits of the field.

Anonymous

Harvest Moon was edited by Ted Rulseh; Chuck Petrie, editor-in-chief. Design and production by Mary Shafer.

ISBN 1-883755-00-X

© 1993 by Lost River Press
P.O. Box 1381
Woodruff, WI 54568

CIP Data

Harvest moon : a Wisconsin outdoor anthology / compiled by Ted Rulseh;
    edited by Chuck Petrie
        p.   cm
    ISBN 1-883755-00-X : $19.95
    1. Hunting--Wisconsin--Anecdotes.   2. Fishing--Wisconsin--
    Anecdotes.   3. Outdoor life--Wisconsin--Anecdotes.   I. Rulseh,Ted.
    II. Petrie, Chuck.
    SK33.H335   1993
    799' .09775--dc20   93-34452
                                                                CIP

I dedicate this book to two men who helped me appreciate the outdoors and outdoor writing: my father, Roger D. Rulseh, and Read W. Eldred.

T.J.R. August 1993

Acknowledgments

Many people helped bring this book into being, but I am especially grateful to Wisconsin's outdoor writers for having enough faith in me to submit material and for offering advice and encouragement when I needed it, which was often. Special thanks to Richard Behm, Scott Bestul, John Beth, Robert Hillebrand, Harvey Imbeau, Don Johnson, John Schroeder, Dan Small, Ed Walker, Jerry Wilber and Galen Winter.

I also thank Earl and Joan Little, Kevin Naze and the Wisconsin Outdoor Communicators Association (WOCA) for welcoming me into the fold and letting me introduce the project to the group's membership.

I am forever indebted to Chuck Petrie, whose unsolicited advice in the early stages helped keep the project on track, and who eventually arranged for publication with Lost River Press.

Finally, I thank my wife, Noelle, and my children, Sonya and Todd, who helped out in ways too numerous to mention, and who got far less attention than they deserved during the eighteen months it took to put this book together.

Ted J. Rulseh
August, 1993

Contents

Contents

Foreword

The idea of this book was born on an airliner cruising at thirty thousand feet, somewhere between Oakland and Milwaukee. Flying home from a business trip, I had just read an outdoor magazine handed to me by a flight attendant.

After scanning the usual articles about how to jig for walleyes and cast for pike in the early spring, I found a story of a flycaster wading a western stream in March, seeking his first trout of the year. Icy water and wind-driven snow made the fishing arduous and unproductive, but the man left satisfied, remembering the look of the stream, an ethereal blue-green he called "the color of hope."

As I closed the magazine, I knew that blue-green trout stream would stay with me forever, perhaps springing to mind while I toughed out an Opening Day cold front on some Wisconsin lake. I felt richer for having read the story, far more so than if I were to use the piece on jigging for walleyes to fill a bag limit.

The outdoor stories that stay with us, I thought, are those that get beyond or around the mechanics of the chase. Then why, I wondered, are such stories hard to find? Half-reclining in my tipped-back chair, I rejected the notion that there were too few gifted writers. No, more likely there were too few outlets. Well, then, I thought, looking out the fuselage window at the patchwork farm fields of the Great Plains, Why don't I create an outlet?

The idea for this anthology took shape on its own momentum, and within a few weeks I began sending letters to Wisconsin's outdoor writers, asking for contributions.

Maybe you'd like to try something longer than the standard magazine piece, I wrote. Perhaps you have a great story turning over in your head but haven't set it to paper because it doesn't fit the popular patterns. Perhaps you already have such a story sitting in your file.

The letters went out and the replies came back, a surprising number saying, "It just so happens . . ." In the end, the hard part was not finding enough excellent material for the collection, but deciding which pieces to include.

On these pages, you'll find favorite selections from the late Mel Ellis, Dion Henderson, Aldo Leopold and Gordon MacQuarrie, four men who built this state's tradition of fine outdoor writing. You'll also find the works of George Vukelich, Clay Schoenfeld, Justin Isherwood, Fran Hamerstrom, and other gifted writers, in whom that tradition carries on.

Perhaps more gratifying, though, are stories from writers just starting to build their reputations or, until now, unknown in outdoor writing circles. It all goes to prove that now, as ever, the craft of outdoor writing thrives in Wisconsin.

Beyond that, each of these stories, in its own way, gets to the heart of why we treasure our time outdoors. Each offers something – a picture, a thought, a memory, a color – to recall on our own outdoor adventures, and so be just a little richer.

ॐ

About the Illustrators

Sharon Anderson, born and raised on a central Wisconsin farm, has focused her talents on wildlife art since being encouraged to do so more than a decade ago by the late Owen J. Gromme, long recognized as the country's dean of wildlife art. She is one of two artists in the nation celebrated for using the "freehand" airbrush method of painting.

Anderson has 35 limited edition prints in circulation, 7 of which have sold out. Her work has graced the covers of many sporting magazines, such as *Wisconsin Sportsman, Michigan Sportsman, and Pennsylvania Outdoors.* She has also designed mirrors, collector steins and paintings that were used to raise funds for various wildlife conservation organizations. Her latest project is a series of six collector plates commissioned by the prestigious Franklin Mint.

Paul Birling is a veteran professional illustrator, presently residing in Appleton, Wisconsin. He has been a contributing artist to several outdoor magazines, including *Wisconsin Sportsman* and the *Wisconsin Outdoor Journal,* for years. His work has also appeared in several other books about wildlife and the outdoors.

Paul is renowned for his distinctive style of line illustration, particularly his evocative, multi-image "collages," which have also appeared in children's books, elementary school textbooks, business communications and advertising.

Jim Goetz is a native of Wisconsin, a child of the Depression for whom many of the stories in this publication have great meaning. Raised and educated in Stevens Point, he graduated from the University of Wisconsin there, with time out for military service during the Korean war. He began his professional career as a teacher in Marshfield. After seven years he changed direction, following a lifelong interest in art into the field of graphic design.

His next 27 years were spent as a freelance commercial artist in the Stevens Point area, doing layout and design, and illustration. A small-town boy at heart, Jim's retirement brought a move to Minocqua with his wife, Nell, and a chance to devote time to his favorite medium, watercolor.

His paintings may be seen in galleries in Minocqua, Ashland, Stevens Point, the Wisconsin Dells and Door County, as well as in various shows throughout the state. Occasional commercial assignments still trickle in, and along with a bit of fishing and time spent with three grandchildren, they manage to keep Jim reasonably content and out of trouble.

Sandy Klein Stevens was born in southern Wisconsin in 1963. As a young girl, she often visited the northern part of the state with her family, staying in her father's cabin deep in the woods. It was there she learned to appreciate wildlife and to love the outdoors.

Graduating in 1985 with a Bachelor's degree from the Kansas City Art Institute, Sandy worked as a graphic designer there for several years before joining her future husband, Mike, in her beloved northwoods. In 1992, she opened Stevens Point, a studio and gallery, in Mercer. Best known for her unique style of pen-and-ink crosshatching, she has developed a reputation for fine art and illustration centered on wildlife and equine subjects. Her color and black & white work has been featured on posters, notecards and sportswear by many organizations including the Logging Congress, Vilas County Historical Museum, the Musky Classic, and the Timber Wolf Alliance.

Walt Sandberg was born in a tiny town in Marinette County and has remained close to home ever since. "When I'm traveling away too long," he says, "I suffer what I've come to understand as withdrawal symptoms. The only thing that can set me right is a quick fix of the northwoods."

Sandberg has many interests but only a few passions: ruffed grouse hunting and whitetail deer hunting; tending 40 acres, a cabin and a trout pond in Oconto County; and stream fishing for brook trout.

His idea of finding what it must feel like to win the Super Bowl is to creel a five-pound brook trout. He has pursued that phantom trophy in northeastern Quebec, the Algoma Country of Ontario, Michigan, Wisconsin and elsewhere. So far, it has eluded him.

Sandberg and his wife, Carol, have twin daughters and seven grandchildren, all of whom are outdoor enthusiasts and call the northwoods home.

That elusive brook trout? "I've heard about a secluded stream that flows into Hudson Bay," he says. "And next July, just after ice-out . . ."

Moonrise On The Avedon
by
Walt Sandberg

L et me take you where you've never been before. Let me take you to the Avedon.

I've fished it often when the misty twilight rolls through the pinetops and the probing fingers of the moon search its silent hidden valley.

I know it, although I do not know it well. Not many do; it's hard to find. The Avedon is a mysterious and secluded trout stream which feeds life into the headwaters of the wild Popple River beyond the reach of many anglers.

Few today can even remember its lilting name, taken from an

immigrant Scottish family that lost its dreams along the Avedon's infertile, rock-strewn banks a generation or more ago.

Today, painstakingly built remnants of that futility still remain: tiny meadows hand-hewn from the virgin forest, outlines of squat fieldstone fencerows now hidden under encroaching trees, a family burial plot, and the memory of a lilac.

What backbreaking labor must have created this place. What hopes must have inspired the builders. How dreadful it must have been to cull a field of stone each spring to make way for a crop which, at best, would be too sparse to feed a hardy family.

And how painful it must have been to finally realize the inhospitable nature of this land and to give it up with family buried in it.

I crossed the homestead to reach my favorite trout lie on the Avedon. And to get there I passed a lilac bush that lived tenaciously in the corner of their meadow.

Each spring it greeted me with fragrant purple blossoms and I reflected: What joy the blooms must have given Mrs. Avedon after the hard, drab winter.

For it was she who had planted the lilac bush, of course. Mr. Avedon, the crusty old Scot, would not have catered to such frivolity – at planting time he would have had more pressing things to do . . . like picking rock.

To get to the trout I must pass a tombstone in the corner of their shrinking meadow. The stone, inscribed with the surname Avedon, marks the resting place of Bryan and Sheila, the immigrants who shared their lives with this isolated soil.

So today, their struggle can be re-created by all who wander here. It's recorded in the purple lilac, in the shrinking meadows, and in the fieldstone fencerows that once pointed my way to the best fishing on the Avedon.

To get to the good fishing, at an extraordinary trout hide that I call Bryan's Bend, I mark my route by Sheila Avedon's lilac bush then turn to travel Bryan's fencerow north. The last stones are dribbled to the streambank and form a rustic armchair which can comfortably accommodate the laziest of anglers. Bryan himself, I think, must have sat upon this same stone chair, after church, to take a Sunday dinner of native brook trout for the Avedon clan.

Some might say that it is not right that I remember the Avedon's harsh and unrewarding history while in search of pleasure. I don't know.

But, I reason, they won't begrudge me for it – so little pleasure they must have had themselves.

I think that's true.

I know that's true.

For once, at moonrise, in early spring, when Sheila's lilac was fairly bursting forth with joy, I sat upon the stony chair and thought I heard a whispering from the forest. "Fish the Lilac Pool," it said. "Fish at Bryan's Bend . . . in the moonlight."

And I thought I detected, too, the rolling of a Scottish brogue in that whispering of the wind.

I fished the Lilac Pool, of course, for – like most anglers – I believe in omens.

But I did not take a fish that night.

The next spring, when I again walked the Avedon in search of the huge brown trout that rose there only in the evening, I plucked, for some unknown reason, a sprig of purple lilac and sought to find the Avedons' remains.

The tombstone was hard to find. I knew it was in the aspen clone at the northeast corner of their dwindling meadow, but this year the opening was smaller – Nature had invaded.

Still, after trodding back and forth, I found the stone. It was choked with newly emerged creeping nettle, wrapped with baby burdock, and tendriled with freshly sprouted hazelnut brush.

I trampled the vegetation down as best I could until the earth before the stone was almost smooth. And gently, with unaccustomed reverence, I placed the lilac sprig.

Then, lighthearted, I went fishing at Bryan's Bend, on Lilac Pool.

That night I fished before the moonrise bathed the Avedon, transforming it into a mystic, fairytale stream. The valley was cobalt black with the shadows of evening and I heard trout smacking insects from the underside of the pool. But none rose to my fly.

Then, just as I was about to quit this most pleasant of pastimes I heard, again, that now-familiar whispering from the trees:

"Fish where the moonlight parts the water," the whisper said.

Where the moonlight parts the water?

I cast my fly – a huge, showy White Miller – precisely at the interface of shadow and moonlight.

And I took a fish. Then another! And several more.

It was the most unbelievable trout fishing I've ever had. It was ecstasy. On every cast a trout . . . if I dropped the fly accurately at the interface.

Yet if I placed my fly too deeply into the shadows, I would have no strike. Nor could I entice a fish if an errant cast curled the fly too far into the moonlight.

But when I dropped it at the interface, precisely at interface, I always hooked a trout and it was always a good one.

I had fun that spring, fishing in the moonlight, on the Avedon, at Bryan's Bend, on Lilac Pool. And I shall remember it always.

I have to remember how it was. For Sheila Avedon's lilac, with its fragrant purple blossoms that herald spring, and Bryan Avedon's streamside fishing chair, are no more. They were cleared away last summer to make room for a widely advertised plat of vacation homesites. Insightfully, the developer's advertising agency has chosen to call it "Whispering Valley."

The Avedon is still there, of course. And so is the tombstone.

But the lilac bush is gone . . . bulldozed under for Lot 17.

Still, I often visit Lilac Pool and Bryan's Bend at twilight, when the moonlight anoints my holy waters.

But it's not the same.

I no longer have the desire to cast a fly at Bryan's Bend now that the banks are denuded and the quarry is hatchery-raised. And I no longer hear the whispering from the forest in that distinctive Scottish brogue, nor can I gather a sprig of purple lilac in the spring to honor Sheila Avedon.

The last, perhaps, is what saddens me most of all.

— *Jim Goetz*

Robert Hillebrand, of Oconomowoc, is father of Jenni, Jessica and Zak, who "tend a San Diego shipyard, travel with a carnival and can change the ribbon in my typewriter, respectively." He is stepfather to Kris and Karin and husband of Sandy, copyreader and "one of the two best cooks on the block."

Born in Lake Mills, he attended college at Marquette and the University of Wisconsin-Milwaukee. He taught high school English for 12 years, then taught composition for 24 years at Waukesha County Technical College.

Hillebrand has published two novels, a college composition text, a dozen short stories, a couple hundred poems and many newspaper and magazine pieces. Now retired from teaching, he contributes regularly to the Milwaukee Journal, the Waukesha Journal and the Oconomowoc Independent, reviews books for Booklover, and also reviews jazz records. His poetry appears in Wisconsin Academy Review, Wisconsin Poet's Calendar and other collections. He describes himself as a "failed athlete and musician but a devotee of sports, music, theatre, books and food; hiker, swimmer, skater, gardener, forager, beer drinker,and watcher of birds,beasts, and the weather."

What We Should Have Done
by
Robert Hillebrand

Back in the thirties when I was six, seven, eight, going on ten, I traipsed along behind my old man to riverbanks, marshes, the lakeshore and the woods, braving wet feet, cold ears and chigger bites, getting lost, being found and learning, bit by bit, season by season, that when it came to the real life of hunters, fishermen and trappers, he and I were outside the loop.

"To be sure," as Gopher Ryan, an undisputed deadeye, put it one brisk autumn afternoon as he presented my father with a pheasant feather, "nobody deserves it less." He'd bagged the bird on a backup shot after the old man had missed again. When Gopher offered me a plume, I shuffled back, shaking my head.

"Take it!" he said, glaring at me as if he were still sighting down a gun barrel, and I marched forward and did. Gopher's brother Al cocked his head off to one side, the way he did when he thought he had something funny to say, and speculated that perhaps my dad was too kindhearted to draw a bead on one of his feathered friends. Suddenly Gopher stopped, pointed at the side of an abandoned barn we were ambling past and shouted, "See if you can hit that, Frankie!"

I wished my old man had the guts to tell him to go to hell, but he snapped to, raised the gleaming twelve gauge he'd taught me to clean but wouldn't yet let me fire, took aim and blasted away. When Gopher, Al, and Shadow Goggins pretended they couldn't hear the shot rattling off the boards, my old man chuckled and tried to wink at me. But I turned to see what Shadow made of all the clowning. He was my hero, a lean, brown, quiet man, a fabled tracker and the best shot of the bunch, a mink rancher who smelled like one. He took no guff from anyone, never laughed, and his hard gray eyes rarely showed what he was thinking. What I thought was that my old man would eat a toad if he figured it would win him points with the men my mother called The Mosquito Inn Gang.

What I should have done was tell my father she was right to complain that we were wasting our time hanging out with that crew of gallivanters. "Some friends!" she said. "Some example they set, those packrats!" She claimed they left their wives, if they still had wives, to poke around in washtubs full of dirty clothes they'd scattered in their wake; and off they rambled, smoking, drinking, gambling, knocking God's birds out of the sky, yanking His fish out of the waters, tormenting the squirrels and the damp-eyed deer.

When she was ranting, my dad always let her run on for a stretch before reminding her that if the wild animals belonged to God, so did the livestock. He drew tears once when he mentioned all the pork chops she'd tucked away, the fish fries she'd held her own at, the chicken dinners she'd served. Then he got a queer light in his eyes and told her, "It's to make a man out of him."

Having heard that blather before, she snorted, clamped her hands to her hips and switched her apron; but in the end she went for it, the hungry way he mussed my hair, the way he repeated: *To make a man.* Whatever it meant, that had a ring to it until it flew by once too often.

Mosquito Inn was a ramshackle cabin off a dirt road a couple miles north of our little lake town, and the guys who gathered there were mostly goodtimers who worked alongside my old man at the dairy equipment factory. They were a hodgepodge: a few bums, a few rounders and a sampling of solid citizens. One of them, gray-haired Emil Pederson, was so fastidious he could have passed muster at an old maid's tea party.

It was Emil who gifted me with his back copies of *Field and Stream.* Each month my dad would bring one home, and after I'd read everything, front to back, he'd study the ads and order curiosities he thought would impress the gang. I still keep in a cigar box on the shelf over my desk the combination compass, can opener and waterproof matchbox that infuriated my mother when she intercepted it in the mail.

In 1940, when the old man turned forty, I scribbled a letter to the editor to let him know how much I enjoyed a story about a bloody bear hunt and to hint that before long I might be following in the author's footsteps, over fields, through the streams, into dark forests and then back to the typewriter I expected to own, some day soon. When *Field and Stream* printed the letter the week before Christmas, I took it for a sign, and so did my old man, who slipped a brand new Royal Portable in a nifty fiberboard case under the tree. Wherever a sixty-dollar-a-week welder found money for such a present was, according to my mother, the great mystery of her life, so far.

Christmas afternoon the old man and I tramped out onto Rock

Lake through a gentle snowfall, fat flakes pinwheeling past our slitted eyes. When he spotted the rickety chicken coop that Gopher and Al had fashioned into an ice-fishing shanty, my father made a beeline for it. I scuffed along behind, and as soon as we'd ducked under the canvas flap he started jabbering about how we'd be seeing ourselves in print once I kicked my new typewriter into gear.

Al and Gopher tipped red faces up from holes in the ice to goggle at him as he tugged out his wallet and extracted the magazine tear-out with my letter. "Don't guess you've seen this," he said, interrupting his spiel to offer the page to Gopher, who snatched it with a mittened paw, turned it over twice and thrust it back.

"'Have now, Frank. You're scarin' the fish!"

I ushered the old man out and bobbed along behind as he shuffled off toward the south shore. A wind had sprung up, and loose snow was shawling up around our galoshes. Occasional flakes still tumbled out of the brightening sky and kept landing in the old man's eyes, and he nearly led us into a big square gap of open water left by the ice house crew.

We scrambled up the embankment to the railroad bridge, he poking holes through the snow and into the gravel to make tiny steps I could set my feet onto, and together we stood on the trestle, staring down until what sounded to me like hounds barking rocked our heads back. Two nearly perfect chevrons of Canada geese scudded low beneath the thinning clouds, one northbound, the other south. They were so close I could see their white chokers and their black feet tucked up under their tails and I felt the wingbeats inside my chest.

"*Her-ONK! A-RONK! Ker-RONK!*" I yelled back. My father laughed out loud as the southbound flight soared up, as if it had hit a bump, spooking those heading the other way.

"Too bad the guys are missing this," he said.

I said nothing, but I was wishing the ice would melt under their bottle of Old Overholt and that Gopher and Al would sink to the bottom like lost fish bait. If not for them, I'd never have been asked to choke down turtle soup or wild duck peppered with buckshot at Mosquito Inn game feeds.

On the other hand, I'd never have been sprung from my bed after midnight to chase after coonhounds, stumbling through swamp water, hopping bogs, dodging moonshadows, keeping my fingers crossed, hoping my dad wouldn't do something dumb. A mixed bag is what it was, and I never took time to sort out the good from the bad while it was happening.

If I wished hard enough, we now and again managed to survive an outing without disgracing ourselves. The safest expeditions were those we set off on alone, for a Saturday morning saunter around the lake or a night walk out beyond the lights of the town, picking out constellations, watching for falling stars, listening to crickets, gawking once when the northern lights towered in great, swirling columns ahead of us.

Using a finger and a thumb, I punched out grade school theme assignments on my new typewriter, embroidering fantasy upon our adventures, coloring the horizon, casting my father as a shadowy figure in the background, dropping a brace of mallards into his game sack, which, had I stuck to the truth, must remain empty, always.

River fishing was, if he had one, the old man's strong suit, and one Saturday afternoon, late, Al Ryan trailed us in his pickup when we drove out to the Crawfish River near what had once been my grandfather's farm. For a couple hours our cane poles stuck out straight over the muddy water, propped by forked sticks the old man had cut. No one got a nibble except Al, whose head began to tilt after he muscled in a big carp and threw it back. Gunny sacks, knotted at their frayed tops with binder twine, lay flat beside us.

Sunset hour the old man trotted out a story I'd heard a dozen times, about his father and how as he grew old he turned greedy, traded in the outdoor life for the nightlife, wooed wild ladies in the roadhouses with his concertina and then spluttered out early. A rover no more, all he could do was rock on the farmhouse porch, staring with half-blind eyes at the sun going down behind the hill in his back pasture.

"He'd be facing west, the old squeeze-box in his lap, until the sun dropped out of sight and then, if he could get up the gumption, after two strokes and all, he'd hump himself up to the top of the ridge, hurrying slow, to watch it set a second time off to the west. That's how greedy he still was.

"Not long after this one was born," said my dad, patting my shoulder, "he was at it again and just before he reached the top he paused, scratching at his chest, tumbled over and came rolling back toward the porch."

"Oh, sweet Jesus!" said Al, clamping his hand over his heart until he needed it to grab a pole that was running away. The bull-heads were swarming.

"So that's why I'm trying to bring up the kid here to be a man, don't you know?"

Al didn't answer because we were all too busy with the poles. When my father called time-out to set fire to the pile of driftwood he'd rounded up earlier, the gunny sacks were bulging. He unwrapped three skinning boards, two feet long, seven or eight inches wide, with a spike sticking up at each end and showed Al, as he'd shown me before, how to impale a bullhead through the head, cut the skin around the gills, slit the yellow belly, gouge out the guts with a thumb and strip away the black skin with a pair of pliers.

"Neat-oh!" yipped Al, falling to like a veteran.

There were enough pliers and knives to go around. I was praying we'd come up short and sneaked off to the bushes to fritter away a few minutes, but when I edged back to the fire there were still plenty of wriggling fish. I slapped a fat one onto the spike, and got sick.

"Some kids, they got weak stomachs," Al allowed, not near so bothered by my performance as my crestfallen father. While they finished up, I toted bags of fillets to the milk cans Al carried in back of his truck. They'd had chunks of ice in them when we parked; it was icy water when I dumped in the cleaned bullheads. While we were packing up, Al volunteered to stow the cans in the ice house until Monday, when he and the old man would be hosting a fish fry at Mosquito Inn. I didn't get invited.

Whenever I tried to get a handle on what set the real outdoorsmen apart from the would-be's like my father and me, I got stuck. Guys I pegged as the genuine article came in all sizes, shapes and styles, like Gopher and his brother – fat and skinny, neat and raggedy, mean-eyed and mellow – or Shadow Goggins and his son Floyd, who both wore hooded sweatshirts and gym shoes. Gopher's red-and-black flannel shirts came from Sears Roebuck, but once he pulled them on, they belonged to him. Al made do with bib overalls, blue work shirts, and a green baseball cap. The aroma from the mink ranch helped to mark Shadow as the real thing, but Emil Pederson was authentic, too, and he smelled of Lifebuoy soap, even on a hot day in the uplands.

My old man believed it had to do with the way you looked and he was always buying himself, and sometimes me, camouflage vests, mackinaws and canvas hats with trout flies for decorations. Once he rigged himself out in high-top boots with rawhide laces and little leather patch pockets for carrying knives and junk, and Shadow told him he looked like a walking satchel. Another time he mail-ordered a bandolier with narrow pouches for shotgun shells, and I had to stand sentinel so that my mother wouldn't seize it. Watching him arrange it over his shoulder in front of my bedroom mirror, I saw his face collapse. Even he could see it was too much, so we hid it in an old wooden box in the outbuilding.

For me, the hikes we took around Rock Lake were better than hunting or fishing. If the old man's outfits embarrassed me, I could always run ahead, lag behind or hide in the underbrush. In spring the gentians popped out on the hillsides, in fall we collected hickory nuts, and in February, for my mother's birthday, we always cut pussywillows with an ivory-handled hunting knife the old man paid an arm and a leg for at Sam's Hardware.

Most of the homes in town, then, were on the northeast side of the lake. From our house it was a two-block walk to Lakeshore Drive, where we turned south, fell back to get around Doc Leicht's red brick mansion, passed behind a few other fenced-in homes and picked up a dirt trail leading through a mile-long stretch of woods. Tent City, where some of the high school kids camped during the summer, was smack dab in the middle.

Once out of the woods, we came up against the chain-link fence enclosing Sandy Beach Resort and were forced to skirt around it to reach the marshland on the other side, which we threaded through until we arrived at the railroad tracks leading to the bridge. Under it flowed a channel connecting Rock Lake to a boggy kettle hole covered with a lid of waterlilies and surrounded by swampland that drove us back whenever we tried to make the circuit. Sometimes, leaving my dad to smoke his pipe on the trestle, I slipped down to the shoreline and tried again.

There I saw snapping turtles, a red-tailed hawk riding the last black branch of a dead tamarack and, once, a blue heron. Not twenty yards away, it gawked like a clown in a dream, and as I crept out from cattail cover our eyes slammed together, its left, my right. As the line over which our two eyes met pulled tight as a wire, I almost called out for my father. Then the great bird snapped the cord, took one long stumbling step, unfurled impossible wings, shattered the still air with two broad, futile-seeming strokes, blustered free and flew.

We veered off the railroad tracks onto the western shore, and a neat little stile that looked like a bench for dolls took us up and over a barbed wire fence and into a cow pasture. A cow or two sometimes strolled along with us until we arrived at the second stile, a good half mile down the strand. Up we stepped, out of the pasture, down we tripped onto the rollercoaster path through Shorewood Hills, a wide belt of virgin timber, mostly pine and spruce, that broke off abruptly at Albright's Orchard, whose long, wavering rows of apple trees ended where the town park began. There, we rested at a picnic table, poked around in the stone fireplaces and drank from a pump with a handle that squeaked.

The northeast shore was the beginning of the end. Most of the elegant new houses there had fences running right down to the edge of the water, so we dropped back out of sight of the lake and for the last mile padded along the blacktop with its view of garage doors and garbage cans.

One Fourth of July weekend when most of the Mosquito Inn crowd had motored to the Upper Peninsula to reel in the lunkers – and the old man was left to "mind the store," as Gopher phrased it – my dad and I started off on a lakeshore promenade and almost stumbled over another stay-at-home, little Floyd Goggins, who was sitting under an oak at the far edge of Tent City, puffing on a bent cigarette. As soon as my father told him we were walking around the lake, he hopped up and led the way. At the Sandy Beach fence he said, "Climb or wade?"

The old man was still spluttering out his explanation of why we had to walk around when Floyd shinnied over and dropped down inside. I waded around to join him, and we zigzagged through the grounds, kicking at the sides of rental rowboats, ogling the slant-legged girls sprawled out on bright beach towels.

"Switch," Floyd called out at the far fenceline. He waded, I climbed, and together, grinning, we waited for the old man to catch up.

Floyd's route kept us closer to the water than we'd managed on our own, and he barely hesitated when we came up against the first fence on the northeast shore. Inside, a scruffy black dog with red eyes and upright ears was pacing peevishly, crouching to spring as Floyd grabbed a picket.

"Careful!" my dad shouted.

"C'mon," Floyd said. "If he bites us the owner'll be sorry." Over he vaulted, and up jumped the dog, to lick his face. My father grabbed my wrists and towed me off to the blacktop.

Back home we found Floyd sitting on our front stoop, smelling faintly of tobacco smoke and the mink ranch, his long yellow hair spiking out from under the stocking cap he wore, winter or summer. My old man fetched a bottle of root beer from the ice box and three mugs. Floyd drained his in one tip-up, stood, turned his hard gray eyes on mine and declared, "If you don't hug the shore, it don't count. You might as well stay home." And then he was gone.

Later that summer my old man's four-dollar bid on a brass telescope with a wobbly tripod and a packet of sky charts held up, and night after night, if the weather was clear, we tried matching the patterns on the charts with what we saw overhead. When the newspaper gave notice that meteor showers might be visible one August evening, my dad spread the tidings at work, and about ten on the promised night we drove out to Mosquito Inn with pans of food he'd talked my mother into fixing. Only Emil, Al and a new guy at the factory showed up.

The old man mounted the telescope on a knoll, and we sat in the clearing, tucking away baked beans and potato salad and gnawing on a stick of venison sausage Al pulled out of his back pocket and passed around. When it was time for the sky to start showing its stuff, each of us took a couple turns peeking through the lenses.

The sky was clear and my father had the telescope lined up as the newspaper had directed, but no stars whizzed by.

"Come out you little buggers," he said, talking to the stars. "It's time!"

The others just trooped inside to play sheepshead, and the old man and I were alone in the moonshine with two empty oven pans and a brass tube.

Soon it was time for the opening of pheasant season, and we

were supposed to meet the gang at a deserted farmhouse twenty miles north of town. Following a penciled map, we located a place with boarded-up windows and a broken windmill, but no one was there. The old man and I strode out into the uplands, circled a weedy field and never flushed a bird.

"The guys must've gone off to try another place," he said, looking stung.

Nearly back to the car, he spotted a flock of sparrows hopping about in a bush. He dropped to one knee and sighted so long, so determinedly, that I could see his upper teeth digging into his lower lip. At last he pulled the trigger – *BUH-LAM* – and tumbled over at the recoil. Under the bush we found one tiny bird, splattered with bright-red blood, twitching and chittering its last.

"Oh, Lord," my old man said. He kicked loose a piece of sod, hollowed out a little grave with the toe of his boot, tapped the sparrow into it and covered it up.

I guess he gave away the shotgun; I never saw it again. Months later I manufactured a story describing him as he flew into a rage, smashed the gun on a rock, jammed the pieces into a culvert and forswore the outdoor life; but – to speak the truth – those things never happened.

We still hiked and fished and tagged along with Gopher and the gang for an occasional hunt, and still I clung to a fuzzy notion of growing up to become an outdoor writer. I entertained my teachers with tales portraying myself as a woodsman. They recognized it for the hokum it was, but when one of them scrawled "Pretty Good" at the top of a coon hunting story, I mailed it to *Field and Stream*. I got it back fast. After that, briefly, I turned my attention to typing romantic poetry meant for the brown eyes of a new girl in my class. She had crow-black hair that swept back from her forehead like wings, and her mysterious see-saw name was Bluebell Schmidt.

The aftermath of Pearl Harbor brought a government contract to the dairy equipment factory and – surprise – one day the old man bumbled in with a shine of glory in his eyes and told us he'd been named first foreman of the welding department.

During the war the plant ran five and a half days a week, so instead of blundering around in the woods on Saturdays I ran errands, dreaming up routes that would take me past Bluebell's house, and at noon my mother and I strolled downtown. I waited outside the bank while she got started on her shopping. When the old man drove up, he and I cashed his check, then made the rounds, checking store windows, greeting everyone who stepped into range. To the ladies he tipped his faded canvas hat with Gopher's drooping feather still stuck behind the band.

One Saturday we made our usual visit to The Pyramid Cafe and found Gopher, Al, Emil and Shadow sitting around two tables they'd shoved together. Everybody said hello, even before the old man did, but no one invited us to sit. Al's head was tilted, and Emil, who'd stopped sending along his copies of *Field and Stream* after my dad's promotion, nodded courteously until we took stools at the counter.

On our way out, the old man hovered near the tables, but the guys were too busy talking to pay him any mind. I was about to tug at his sleeve when he got underway. Right hand on the doorknob, he turned back and flapped his left. "Try to get along without us," he said to no one listening. Glumly he led us to Sam Kiesow's Hardware, a long, narrow, dusty store, where he and Sam would sit on nail kegs, chewing the fat, trading jokes and perusing old catalogs while I kept an eye out for my mother.

The old man rose out of his funk in a blink when he beheld Sam's new window display. "Now that is what I call fire engine red!" he exclaimed, tapping my shoulder and pointing at a contraption under a sign that read: BE THE FIRST IN YOUR CROWD!

The base was a glossy scarlet box housing a battery. Red metal posts jutted up from the sides to support what I took to be a headlamp from a truck. Connecting lamp to battery were fat black insulated wires, and there was a shiny handle, too, like the ones on gas cans, and a chrome switchplate. My father's eyes reflected everything.

As we scrambled through the doorway, a bell jangled, but as always, the store looked untended. We followed the row of unshaded lightbulbs that dangled low from the high, cobwebbed ceiling and when we stood under the last, there sat Sam, silhouetted against a dirty rear window, leafing through a magazine.

"Morning, Sam."

He flicked a glance at us, big and little, over the top of his page, but said not a word. After a silent minute the old man declared, "Sam, we'd like to take a gander at that fisherman's flashlight you got in your window."

Sam sucked his teeth and, ever so slowly, turned two pages.

"Ain't no flashlight in my window, unless someone snuck one in while my back was turned."

My father laughed, as if he'd just heard the first joke of the day. "It's the red one I mean, if that helps you to place it. It wasn't there last week."

"Ain't been a flashlight there since two years ago last spring when I carried that line of nickel-plated jobs that sold so good."

"C'mon, Sam, I'll show you."

My old man bustled back up the aisle, but Sam sat tight on his nail keg. "If it's that new Camp-Light you're talkin' about, Frankie, haul it on back here. I'll douse the lights and show you what it can do."

I watched my dad hoist the apparatus gingerly out of the display, then stepped outside to wait for my mother, hoping he wasn't going to buy it and duck back to The Pyramid Cafe to show it off. My mother, shifting her weight huffily from foot to foot, smiled when he emerged ten minutes later, empty-handed.

Sunday night we combed the wet grass in the backyard, he with a coffee can, I with a nickel-plated flashlight, collecting nightcrawlers. I stabbed the beam here, there, and he hopped like a frog, pouncing when a worm showed. Now and then he whispered, "Get that one," even though he knew I hated the way they squirmed and tried to hang on when you plucked them from their holes.

"You're gonna have to learn to handle things you don't always like if you want to grow up to be a man." I did want to grow up to be a man, but I wasn't sure what kind of man I wanted to be, other than one who could win the heart of Bluebell Schmidt.

He was late getting home from work Monday, and my mother was at the window when the Ford pulled into the drive. After supper she filled a bag with peanut butter cookies and stepped out to wave us off.

"It'll be dark before you get there."

"The dark doesn't scare us, does it?" I shook my head no.

"You men," she said, laughing at us as if we were boys. I was afraid of the dark and of river snakes and fish guts but I wasn't about to say so.

Once we were out of town, the old man's tight daytime smile loosened up. We parked where we had the time Al came along, near the bridge over the Crawfish. After unloading the poles, he snicked the lock on the trunk, hauled out a big brown package and said, "Open it." I knew what I'd find, another gadget he hoped would knock the socks off the Mosquito Inn Gang, if ever they chanced to see it.

Fire engine red it was, even in the fading light.

"You can carry it."

"Should I switch it on?"

"Not now. I could walk this riverbank blindfolded. You too."

He led, I followed, and the bump of the lantern against my leg felt like a drumbeat. Night clicked down while we were on the path. Even before we saw it, we could hear the river, running high, and when we broke out of the bushes onto the muddy bank, the water licked at our boots. It was our first time out for a while, and

— Jim Goetz

everything looked changed. As we drew near to our spot, the river widened until it was too dark to see the opposite bank. I was stumbling along, scanning the sky for bats when, suddenly, we both jumped at a loud splash from across the river.

"Throw the light on the water!" the old man shouted.

Scared, I spun around and let the Camp-Light fly. My father was leaning out over the river, trying to stare through the dark, when it came down.

PA-LOOSH!

And then I was trying to see his face in the dark, wondering how to explain that I hadn't meant to spite him, that it was a reflex. At the last split second I tried to hang on, but it was too late. After a long, silent time a heavy hand settled upon my shoulder and guided me to the old log we always sat on; as my eyes got used to the dark, I could make out two forked sticks we'd punched into the ground the last time out, and I kept my eyes on them until he cleared his throat.

"You shouldn't have done that," he said plainly.

Moments later I found myself pronouncing the same words, tumbling each one over and clunking it down in its place.

"You shouldn't have done that."

What we should have done was talk, but exchanging words with your father is never easy. I could have told him he was worth more than the whole Mosquito Inn Gang all rolled up together and tied with a ribbon. Maybe he could have explained to me what he was looking for, what he expected. Maybe all he needed was a friend. Too late now.

We never did find out what caused the ruckus across the river. Possibly it was Shadow Goggins wrestling with a snapping turtle. The old man and I sat side by side, as near to one another as we'd ever get, staring straight ahead at the water streaming past.

ॐ

Jerry F. Wilber lives with his wife, Karen, eight-year-old daughter Katie, dog Butch and "assorted chickens, ducks, muskrats, beavers, deer and mosquitoes" on eight wild acres near South Range in northwestern Wisconsin, not too far from the Brule River and not too far from Lake Superior, which he watches from his classroom window.

Wilber has written over 1500 newspaper columns entitled "Wit and Wisdom of the Great Outdoors." His radio program of the same name is heard on numerous stations, five times a week. His first book, also called Wit and Wisdom of the Great Outdoors, was published in fall 1992. His second, Run, Johnny, Run, was published in spring 1993. His short stories have appeared in outdoor magazines throughout the United States and Canada.

Where Have You Been, Papa, And Where Are The Fish?

by

Jerry F. Wilber

Having left the house with the morning light, the fisherman was tired. Having been rained on most of the day, he was wet. Having dropped his lunch into a deeper part of the lake, he was hungry. But having stopped at length at the Double Barrel Saloon to dry out and exchange yarns with old pals, he was not in the least thirsty.

So as a misty daylight finally fades into darkness, an old beat up pick-up truck, loaded with fishing tackle, odds and ends of an all-day expedition on the lake and a much-used fisherman, lurches up the driveway, rumbles to a fitful stop and shudders into silence. An equally used fourteen-foot aluminum boat follows noisily into the yard, stopping obediently behind them.

From a rain-streaked picture window overlooking the front yard, two watch as the fisherman laboriously gathers armsful of rods and reels, tackle box, mosquito repellent, thermos bottle, life jacket, minnow bucket, worm can, seat cushion, extra sweater and fishless stringer. They watch as he unsteadily makes his way up the path to the front door.

One who watches, the much taller of the two, frowns as she anxiously grips her bowling ball and nervously glances at her watch. She is late for the Wednesday night ladies' league in town.

The other, much smaller but carrying the same dark eyes and hair as her mother, clutches a raggedy doll named Margaret, presses her nose against the window and giggles as her father, seeing them standing there, doffs his lucky fishing hat and, bowing like a gallant knight from her storybook, drops the tangled load in his arms into a tangled heap on the lawn.

He studies the pile at his feet for a moment, then, assuming the posture of a defeated though proud general, he marches toward the door behind which lies warmth, comfort and love.

For the most part.

As he doodles with the doorknob to get the thing turning in the right direction, the door opens abruptly, nearly causing him to lose his regal balance. And he comes face to face, nose to nose with the love of his life, who sweeps by him with a contemptuous look and disappears into the darkness to join the girls at the Allouez Bowl.

They are alone together then, the two of them – three counting Margaret, and Margaret certainly counts. He, the father, nearly filling his end of the hallway; she, the daughter, just a little part of hers; until, like an old movie, they move toward each other, and he swings her high and hugs her deep into his coated arms smelling damply of lakes and woods and high adventure and more than a hint of the Double Barrel Saloon.

She is filled with clean, little girl, bedtime smells of soap, shampoo and toothpaste, and she hugs him hard back, but doesn't like the day-old growth of whiskers on his face and turns up her nose like you-know-who.

"Did you catch lots of fish today, Papa?" There is excitement in her voice.

"Where's supper, Pumpkin?" Gruffly. He doesn't want to talk about it.

She hesitates, confused, "In the oven, Papa." They always *ooh* and *aaah* over each and every fish he catches, first thing. "Should I get supper for you, Papa?"

"No, Cucumber." The top of her head comes about even with the top of the stove. "You put papa's coat away." He puts her down, and she drags the thing to the hall closet.

Without noticeable coordination, he pulls a casserole from the oven, sets it on the counter, slides it around a lone rose surging into the air from a tiny vase, and pushes it to the waiting plate, silver, napkin.

She returns, silently goes to the refrigerator, retrieves a carton of milk, sets it before him and struggles up to a stool opposite her father, her dark eyes large with questions, a trace of a frown lining her forehead.

Broken only by sounds of a hungry man vigorously satisfying his appetite, unencumbered by etiquette, the silence between them drags, begging for a word, a nod. When finally, with his mouth full, his eyes squinting hard, he jabs a fork in her direction, his voice challenging.

"Do you really want to know what went on out there today?"

She blinks, swallows hard, nods cautiously.

"Okay." His voice is heavy with warning and tuna hot dish, which he hates. "But don't say I didn't warn you."

"I won't, Papa." It is nearly a whisper, but from her, a solemn promise.

"Well, if you're sure then . . ." He eyes the unfinished casserole, shrugs, refills the plate.

She crosses her arms on the counter and rests her chin there. Margaret leans against a bowl of apples, button eyes watching.

"I get to the lake, see, and it's as dark as the basement with the lights off. A thick, gloomy fog sits heavy on land and water alike.

35

Then from somewhere in the trees behind me, I hear a weird noise. *Whooo. Whooo. Whooo.*"

With her father's mournful cry the little girl shivers; the hair on the back of her neck tingles. He shakes his head.

"It was probably the ghost of an old Indian chief who carries his head under his arm and on dark, foggy nights walks up and down the shore trailing a deer he wounded two hundred years ago. *Whooo. Whooo.* The sound comes closer and closer."

"What ever did you do, Papa?" She can see it all.

"Oh, Junebug, I can tell you I put that boat in the water right away and scooted to the middle of the lake."

"That's good, Papa." She is relieved.

"Not so good, Tomato. I was trolling up and down the lake. Up and down. Up and down. And I didn't get one single bite."

"That's too bad, Papa."

"Not so bad, Sunflower, because after a couple of hours a great big fish grabs my hook, so I shut off the motor and start to reel him in."

"Oh boy! How big, Papa?" This is what she has been waiting to hear.

He lets out a long sigh and shakes his head again.

"About as big as a cow."

"No!"

Margaret keels over.

"Yes. It had big ugly eyes, a tail bigger than a shark's and a mouth with a million teeth. It was so big it started to pull me and the boat around and around the lake. Around and around we went making waves taller than you."

"Papa, how long did you do that?" She shivers again.

He yawns, "Rosebud, let's go into the den and build a fire."

She has difficulty getting the milk down from the counter, but she manages and puts it in the refrigerator. By the time she gets Margaret and shuts off the kitchen light, her father is hunched over the fireplace in the den, muttering to himself. A fifth match produces a tiny blaze that grows and spreads dancing shadows across the room.

Satisfied, he lies down on the sofa on one side of the fireplace and closes his eyes; she perches expectantly on an overstuffed chair opposite him. And waits.

But this time she can't take it.

"And what then, Papa?"

"What about what, Angel?"

"The fish, Papa, what about the fish!"

"The fish? Oh yes, that was just before the pirates came."

"Not pirates, too, Papa?"

"Yes, Peanut. As I was about to put the fish in my net I looked up, and coming around the island was a mean-looking ship loaded with mean-looking pirates." He yawns again.

"Were they for-real pirates, Papa?"

"You better believe your papa knows pirates when he sees them, Sweetheart. They had brown uniforms with patches on the sleeves; they carried guns, wore wide-brimmed hats and had shiny badges on their chests."

"And then what, Papa?" What a brave, wonderful father she has.

"And then with no warning at all, the sky turned black and it started to storm."

"And a storm too, Papa!" She is desperate. "What about the poor fish?"

"There I was," his voice a hoarse whisper, "a whale pulling me around the lake, trying to eat me, pirates closing in at any second, wind blowing a hundred miles an hour, lightning flashing everywhere, thunder booming, rain coming down by the bucketsful, a headless ghost waiting for me on shore . . ."

Silence.

"Papa?"

Nothing.

"Are you sleeping, Papa?"

There is only even, contented breathing.

She sighs, climbs down from the chair, moves to the lamp on the desk and shuts it off.

Clouds have gone, stars dimly sprinkle the sky, and the moon begins to climb above the balsams down by the garden as the car pulls into the driveway and stops. The driver gets her bowling ball from the back seat and a pretty good score card from the dash.

She intends to walk around the pile of fishing junk still on the path to the house, but instead untangles each piece as carefully as she can and carries them to the garage, placing each neatly on the workbench there. Except for the worm can.

She eases herself from the dark night into the dark house. She flips on the hall light and sighs as she stoops to pick up an old coat that couldn't make it into the closet and hangs it next to her own.

In the kitchen she puts dirty dishes in the sink, wipes the counter clean, ignores, for the time being, a dried out casserole dish.

On her way past the den she stops, and in the soft light carried by a new moon, studies the fisherman and their daughter stretched out side by side with Margaret, on the sofa, breathing deeply, sleeping soundly.

She smiles to herself, covers them with an afghan she made last Christmas, and tip-toes off to bed.

&

— Sandy Klein Stevens

Scott Bestul is a Wisconsin native who now lives in Lewiston, Minnesota. Bestul's connections with his home state remain strong. He continues to deer hunt on family land near Iola (the setting for "Eben's Eyes"). He also bowhunts for deer and turkeys in Buffalo County, and fishes for trout on Wisconsin's many rivers.

Scott's wife, Shari, is an elementary school counselor, but he receives most of his therapy while wandering the woods and streams of Wisconsin and Minnesota. His stories have appeared in Wisconsin Outdoor Journal, Sports Afield, Sporting Classics, and Gray's Sporting Journal.

Eben's Eyes
by
Scott Bestul

He was 52 when he learned he could no longer drag out the bucks that he killed. After pulling, then tugging, at one beam of a mahogany six-tine rack, he knew the hundred-yard drag to the logging road was not possible. The yearling lay inert behind him. He was disgusted with himself, but was too out of breath to grumble to the oaks about his failing health. Instead, he shifted a mealy clump of snuff with his tongue, spat onto the snow, and sat down to wait for me.

When I heard his shot, I made my way silently to Eben's rock. Family rumors of the crippling effects of his former three-pack-a-day habit had reached me, and I remembered his slow shuffle toward his stand when I left him that morning. After shaking his hand and turning down a two-dollar bribe, I set to work dressing out the buck. As my frigid hands explored the warm cavity of the deer, I asked Eben to describe his kill.

When he was finished, I made the pull look as difficult as I could for an animal that would dress out at 110 pounds, but I still had to wait for Eben twice before we got to the logging road. He tried to make some joke about being a good still-hunter now, but in his face was a clear, grateful "thank you" that lingered beyond the normal allotment that old Norwegians give for eye contact. I held his stare until he broke it and looked at the yearling on the road beside him.

"Six-year-old," he chuckled, pointing at the half-dozen tines on the basket rack of the buck. I grinned widely at the pleasant recall of the old wives' tale we had both believed at one time in our hunting careers.

Ten years have passed since that day. Today, in the heat of July, I am back with Eben, watching an auctioneer sell what is left of his farm. Emphysema has foreclosed on Eben's operation. I retreat to a shady maple, trying to ignore the humidity, the auction hands, even some of my relatives. But Eben I can watch – moving among the furniture, buyers, and auction hands that clutter his front yard.

A cotton shirt and trousers hang on his frame, and his shoes and hat seem to be the only things that really fit him. The hat is one worn by many men his age: straw, narrow-brimmed, with a multi-colored hatband that is mostly black. He wears it back on his head in an open, honest fashion – it doesn't seem to be there for any purpose, only to attest that he is used to wearing hats. He is also doing something that he has become used to – stopping for a swallow of July air so that he can walk the rest of the distance across his lawn.

A walnut bedroom set in the middle of the lawn is his limit on this sweltering day. As the sounds of bidding increase, Eben sits limply on a boxspring, his legs crossed as he watches an auction hand hold up a metal rooster weathervane. He stares at the bird, mildly interested, but the bidders increase their offers in urgent tones. Eben remains heron-like as I join him on the mattress. His face is as wind- and sun-burned as when I first recall seeing him. Since that time I have always remembered my uncle for his chafed complexion, complete with blue-purple veins that looked like far away rivers on his cheeks.

The bidding for the rooster has become more intense, and, as expected, my father enters the fray, determined to carry out his plan "to drive up the price for those damn antique dealers who don't understand the importance of a family heirloom!" Eben knows my dad wants the weathervane, and the sound of a coarse "seventy-five!" brings a smile to his eyes as they shine from his weathered cheeks. They are hunter's eyes – a pair of maple-bark-grey rovers that miss little, still or moving. I remember telling dad about having to drag the buck for Eben, and wondering aloud whether he would hunt again.

"A man hunts with his eyes and his heart," dad told me, and that was all. I was younger then, and it took me until the next season to really understand what he meant.

I had jumped three deer as I walked toward Eben on a five-man slow drive of our swamp. I ignored black hooves, bobbing flags, and looked between three sets of ears for the horns that must be there for Eben to fill his tag. "Bald, bald, bald," I said to myself as they crashed away. I took a breath of cool swamp air, stood on a hummock, and let my heart slow down. When it did, I let my mind wander out of this drive and into the next in a run of psycho-babble that is the bane of any deer hunter.

"No bucks here. Where next? East woods? Too much pressure. Lindsey 40? No deer in the high ground today. Spruce swamp? Perfect. No one's hit it all week. There's sure to be a buck in the —" My soliloquy was interrupted by a sudden BOOM! that shook me off my high, dry perch into ice-crusted swamp water. It was Eben, I knew, as the echo of the 12-gauge caromed off the trees and marsh grass.

As I walked toward the sound of the shooting, my cousin sloshed toward me, his eyebrows arched in query. "I thought those three were bald," he said. I felt relieved – surely both of us couldn't be wrong. When we reached Eben, he was using the toe of his boot to smooth the fur of a deer that had made it out of the swamp water before it died. Cousin Tom reached down to lift the deer's head by its horn – a spiny, almost-shorter-than-legal knob that neither of us had seen but that had caught Eben's eyes as the buck sprinted through the swamp.

An emphatic *"So-weld!"* brought me away from a one-horned buck and back to a metal rooster that had gone for $200 and, in the process, made my relatives more angry at an antique dealer than when old man Krogewold sold Aunt Ella's rosette irons out of the family at her auction. As "the foreigner" marched up to claim his fowl, Eben's grin reached up to his hatbrim. "Imagine a tin chicken sellin' for that!" he chuckled. Behind him, my dad glared at the winner of the bidding war. Other relatives, in a rare fit of bad humor, were venting their irritation on whatever came up – "the heat, too much dust, auctioneer playin' favorites."

While they groused at each other in tones disguised from anyone outside the family, Eben sat on the boxspring, oblivious. I listened to him breathe, wheezing like a perforated squeezebox. At 62, with emphysema so bad he couldn't walk his yard without stopping, his failing lungs still couldn't keep his eyes from smiling at the thought of somebody paying $200 for a barn ornament.

Eben's eyes had long been a source of fascination for me. We had first become close when I was ten, two seasons before I could hunt but old enough to hang around the gang at noon and walk along on the short drives. Eben emerged from a robust group of hunters as one who I described to my dad as "my friend – the man with eyes like Santa."

My dad chuckled at the comparison, but acknowledged that Eben's eyes were something special. He told me of watching Eben shoot marbles thrown in the air with a .22, or lighting a matchstick placed on a fencepost at 50 feet. When he was young, Eben was given the task of culling the sparrows that tried to move into the martin house in the farmyard, a chore he performed with a pellet gun and very few misses.

I had my own dead-eye story of Eben – was witness to a shot that I wouldn't have believed unless I'd seen it, and would have called it luck if it were anyone other than Eben.

We were posting close to each other on a field edge as the drivers worked the spruce swamp below us. The buck had waited as long as he could in the shelter of the spruce. He was what we have come to call a "Helvetia Township typical" – 18 months old, a low six- or eight-point rack, nerves ready to explode, and enough speed to keep up with the Soo Line for a forty-length. He watched for an opportunity, snuck behind one poster, reached the edge of the swamp, and took off across the plowed field, intent on making the safety of the protective bog on the other side.

Eben was between the deer and me, so I relaxed and watched the beauty of a whitetail deer in full flight. Suddenly, out of the corner of my eye I saw movement, and shifted my gaze to Eben. He held his shotgun at his shoulder, but his head was off the stock, judging distance and speed. I did the same. Seventy yards from me to Eben, 200 to the buck and that increasing every second. Then, with an agonizingly slow movement, his cheek went to the stock. My eyes shifted to the buck as it kicked dirt in an arc behind it. The shot exploded the silence, and I imagined matchsticks on fenceposts and marbles in the air. Eben lowered the gun. The buck continued his streak across the field.

"C'mon, you've got four more," I coached silently. I wanted an Annie Oakley show: five shots, five hits, a deer piling up on itself … Eben began walking toward the deer, the gun cradled in his arm. I looked in time to see the buck make the edge of the bog, rear on its haunches, and fall over backward.

I think about that shot every time we hunt the spruce swamp. It was so simple and yet so deadly, as if the buck's run across the fields was a sentence and Eben's shot the period that ended it. I also think about his eyes – hawk-like, sighting down the barrel, icy and grey. It's funny too, because though it was the best shot I'd ever seen, or ever will see, I don't like to think of it. I like to think of Eben as the man with eyes like Santa, the man who took a 12-year-old into protective custody when his father had some hunting to do, the man who watched me fall crossing a fence with a gun as big as I was, and was gracious enough to hold back the laughter that had to be there.

Later in the day of the fence-falling incident, Eben came up to me and tugged on my sleeve.

"Did ya wanna try a little ice fishing den?" I paused in wonder. Quit deer hunting? There were two hours left! The hunting elders were in a circle, drawing little maps in the snow, planning the next drive. It didn't look like they were too worried about my suggestions on where to place the posters. Eben was in the cab of his truck, winking at me. Feeling like a kid stealing cookies, I ran and hopped in. We chugged off almost unnoticed.

"I like dis better'n drivin' dem swamps any day," he chortled as we bounced down the logging road that led to a secluded lake.

It was a magical two hours. We shuffled out on four-inch ice, sliding and laughing like kids. I carried the buckets, two five-gallon pails with miniature rods and tiny fluorescent jigs inside. Eben carried an iron chisel-rod that punched through the black ice in five strokes, and his Browning, "yust in case." We tipped the buckets over, sat on them, dug waxies out of a used snuff tin and watched little corks blow back and forth across the holes as the wind shifted. I laughed when Eben spat snoose on the ice, challenged him to make a face, and laughed even harder when he did. We watched our corks more intently when mine disappeared once, and when we left I was scrambling on my knees to gather up two dozen pancake-size bluegills as they flopped in the evening shadows.

When we joined the gang back at the cars they were exhausted, chilled, deerless. They peered into our buckets and gaped.

"Looka da sizofum! Geez! Whereja gettim?" We were heroes, he and I. Meat getters. Trophy hunters. I looked at Eben in the glow of the headlights. I saw him wink again, but it was different from the invitation he gave before our expedition. It was an initiation. I belonged.

I felt a tug at my sleeve and was ready to jump in the truck for another ice-fishing trip, but it was Eben's wife reminding us to get off the mattress.

"That's it, you two. Time to head to town."

We got up, Eben and I, watching buyers maneuvering furniture and little gray trunks of junk to their cars. Eben scanned the half-acre lawn helplessly.

"Used ta mow it in two hours," I heard him mumble. It might as well have been a quarter-section for as long as it would take him now. His wife beckoned from the car, inviting him to town, a small apartment, a life with less rigor. Eben wheezed as he walked to the car.

What had been sold, I wondered, as I day-dreamed of a younger, healthier Eben? The little fishing poles and cork bobbers? A walnut-and-steel Browning? I felt a panic rise in me as I thought of the loss of those treasures. I had come today to bid goodbye to Eben's farm, surely, but also to pick up some form of remembrance of him to carry with me to the deer woods this fall. I rushed to the car before Eben made it to the door.

"Eben, I was wondering about deer season this fall. . ." I stopped there. I knew he would feel bad if the rods and gun were gone and couldn't be retrieved. In his eyes, however, flashed a familiar twinkle.

"Yust a minute," he gurgled. He moved to the back of his car, digging in his trousers for a key. The trunk popped open, revealing some old burlap sacks. Eben tossed them aside. A familiar gun case lay on the bottom of the trunk, surrounded by jig poles and ice fishing lures. Eben patted the cased Browning. "I bought my license today," he whispered, looking nervously toward the driver's seat, "and I kept these in case there's ice onna lake!" He winked then, like we were about to leave for the ice and hunt for trophy bluegills.

I experienced a wave of skepticism–remembered his difficult breathing, saw him pause for air in the middle of his lawn. Then, in the back of my mind, I heard my father. "A man hunts with his eyes and his heart."

I saw Eben winking at me from his truck, helping me up after I fell over the fence, sharing my elation at providing a fresh fish dinner for our camp . . . and I felt a spasm of shame. My eyes left the gun and rods in the bottom of the trunk and found Eben's. I winked back, in my best imitation of him – a feeble one I'm sure. I'd never seen anything to match Eben's eyes.

– *Sharon Anderson*

Clay Schoenfeld is a University of Wisconsin-Madison emeritus professor of journalism/mass communication and of environmental studies. He is also an emeritus dean of intercollege programs. Schoenfeld, who first appeared in print as an outdoor magazine writer, is the author, co-author, or editor of 15 books in the fields of outdoor recreation, wildlife management, ecology, and environmental education. In 1981 he was named Conservation Communicator of the Year by the National Wildlife Federation, later serving on its board of directors.

Schoenfeld, of Madison, has been president of the North American Association for Environmental Education and holds its Walter E. Jeske Award. He is now contributing editor of three national newsletters for personnel in higher education, operating from a cabin on 60 acres in Iowa County, the scene of many years of "hunting, fishing, birdwatching, and botanizing."

A veteran of both World War II and the Korean Conflict, he retired as an army reserve infantry colonel in 1975 after having served in the Pentagon as reserve deputy chief of public affairs.

Growing up in Lake Mills, Schoenfeld was a schoolmate of Dion Henderson. As a graduate student, one of his professors was Aldo Leopold. His wife is a former USDA Forest Service naturalist. He has three daughters and eight grandchildren. Of his story, Memorial Day Creek, he says: "Some of it really happened; about the rest I can't say for sure."

Memorial Day Creek
by
Clay Schoenfeld

If Joe Johnson had lived, he would probably have compiled a book like this. Joe had a knack of putting earthy words down on paper – so you could just about smell the shadowed pines at a bend in the river, or hear the spent wings of a downed grouse as they beat on a woodlot floor. He won a writing prize at the University of Wisconsin in 1940, and a couple of Johnson poems appeared in one of those little anthologies back in 1941.

But that's all. Joe is dead. He was the recon officer for a heavy weapons company in the 8th Division. A land mine blew up his jeep early on the morning of June 27, 1944, somewhere south of St. Lo, France.

Some of us are publishing a little volume of the poems and sketches which a battalion chaplain found in Joe's musette bag. In his fashion, Joe speaks for all those men of field and stream who went on the Big Trip and never came back. Joe says what all of them felt: that you carry with you in your heart, forever, a little bit of your outdoors. And your outdoors, in turn, retains a little bit of you.

As Joe wrote:

> *Come what comes,*
>
> *If you want to meet me in the years ahead —*
>
> *You will find me where men tent together;*
>
> *Along a stream the first shy days of any Spring;*
>
> *And where the cornshocks march in ordered rows*
>
> *Against the hazy sky of every Fall.*

There's a sort of a story behind this particular verse of Joe's — a story which I hesitate to tell, because I can't for the life of me decide how much of it is true and how much is pure fancy. Some of it happened, I know, but whether the rest of it is even possible, only Joe can say for sure.

It all began 45 years ago, when Joe and I were growing up in southern Wisconsin. Around the calendar we hunted and fished together whenever school was out — and sometimes when it wasn't. We had a favorite trout stream. It was a little creek that rises in a spring up near Mount Horeb and flows down toward Black Earth. I never have heard of an official name for the stream. Joe and I just called it Memorial Day Creek, because we fished it faithfully every thirtieth of May. Joe was in love with all of outdoor Wisconsin, but I think he liked our creek best of all.

Joe and his stream were a lot alike. A man and his trout creek do grow together somehow, know what I mean? It is beautiful there on a fresh May day with the wind rustling the new leaves on the willows and red-winged blackbirds cheering from spires of alder. Joe's writing was like that. The trout are mostly browns, not big fish but scrappers that lie in the narrow slicks and strike hard. Joe must have soldiered like that, too. The valley is as peaceful and remote as a cemetery, and, come to think of it, the whitened aspens sort of look like tombstones. I guess Joe would feel at ease there right now.

I can still see Joe as he would creep up to a likely spot on his hands and knees and maneuver his fly rod into position. Joe always fished as steady as the current. He would work a single hole for half an hour. As he cast he was always whistling "I'm Always Chasing Rainbows." That was sort of Joe's song, you might say. It was popular in the twenties, you may remember, and Joe liked it. He was still whistling it on Memorial Day of 1941.

We were seniors at the university and we drove out from Madison just to keep our annual date with Memorial Day Creek. He didn't know it at the time, of course, but that was the last time Joe was ever to fish Memorial Day Creek. At least so far as I can say for sure. The next month we went in the Army. We went to Camp Grant together. Joe was sent on to Camp Livingston one afternoon. That's the last time I saw him alive. He's buried in St. Corneille Military Cemetery in France.

I get back to Memorial Day Creek occasionally. As a matter of fact, I was there one recent May 30. I got to the stream about four in the morning, before the sun was all the way up. It was dark and misty, and if I hadn't known every foot of the valley, I wouldn't have been able to start fishing right away. So I was surprised to find somebody already working the opposite bank.

The fellow was down on his hands and knees, casting under a low-hanging willow, and I couldn't make him out in the half light

–Jim Goetz

except to see that he seemed to be wearing an old set of Army fatigues and GI boots. He didn't say anything and I didn't want to disturb the fishing, so I didn't say anything either. Presently, I heard him playing a heavy fish, and then he tramped on downstream, whistling as he went. I worked on up to the spring and back again. By this time the sun was up and the mist gone. I had taken three nice trout and I would just as soon have showed them off to somebody, but I couldn't find the fisher I had run into earlier. He had evidently quit for the day.

It was not until that evening that I made anything peculiar out of my encounter with that fisher in the mist. I had stopped at Joe's home, and Mrs. Johnson had given me an infantry notebook full of Joe's poems. I was reading them over and I came to these haunting lines:

If you want to meet me in the years ahead,

You will find me . . .

Along a stream the first shy days of any Spring . . .

All the old thoughts of Joe came rushing back as I read. You know how it is. Something triggers your memory: Joe shooting squirrels in Ferry's Woods with his .22. Joe catching frogs in Weber's Meadow. And mostly, Joe coming down along Memorial Day Creek, with a string of trout at his belt, whistling as he cast.

And then I remembered: our creek that morning in the dawn. A fisherman on the other side. And the tune he was whistling was "Chasing Rainbows."

❧

Justin Isherwood is a farmer in Wisconsin's Big Sandy, the vegetable growing area in the north center of the state. His great, great grandfather ran the first licensed innhouse on the upper Wisconsin; other forbears were Indian agents, lumberjacks and, as might be expected, sodbusters.

Isherwood began writing in college and has continued ever since to pen nature essays, short stories and a variety of newspaper columns. His wife, Lynn, is a Milwaukee girl he met while canoeing the Boundary Waters. Their daughter, Heather, is a journalism major at Columbia. Their son, Isaac, is a high school senior.

Their farm, near Plover, at the border of the Northern Outwash, is communicant to the Buena Vista Marsh where the return of the sandhill crane heralds the planting season. Each spring the family taps the maple bush as did the grandfathers before, "less for profitability than as an invocation of a farmer's connection with earth, season and blame luck."

For pleasure Isherwood whittles, runs an old-fashioned sawmill, messes with old tractors, but mostly ponders. He wears a kilt, sings baritone, admires trout and places of trout, and drives a 1936 MG roadster with a picnic basket attached. He watches crows and clouds, visits old cemeteries and barns, keeps a microscope atop the player piano, and went to the Amazon to cure his fear of snakes.

Trout Killer

by

Justin Isherwood

Every place worth anything at all has a trout-killer, least every tangle of vegetation and resident stoneboats with enough bone to believe it is real. The term "trout-killer" bothers some folks. I'm sorry for that. The expression isn't very modern or politically correct – an old word, an untamed manner, trout-killer is. Izaak Walton would have recognized the word. It has a clandestine sound, a contrary-to-the-statutes noise, looser than a person ought to be in the present age.

To be frank, "Trout-Killer" as I knew him wasn't what you might call regulation. Just being around him made a body feel a little

outlaw and some pretty ordinary things had a startling new intimacy. I mean woods and creeks and brown bats and nightcrawlers,
the same bunch of stuff nobody else seems the least bit interested in.
What I felt, what we felt in his, I mean the trout-killer's, presence
was gratitude, whether or not we knew what the word meant.

Trout-Killer knew the real name of the English sparrow – it
wasn't even a sparrow – and where the blackberries are ripe without
having to go look. He didn't know much about nuclear physics or in
the Bible whether Isaac was the son of Abraham or Noah or if it was
ten commandments or fifty-two, but he did know where a meadow
of goldenrod had the biggest array of wolf spiders you ever want to
see at once. And where on the Buena Vista Marsh you can sit on a
tamarack dune and, across the scrub, spy on a coyote den.

⁜

Willie was the township's trout-killer. Same as the town had a
chairman, dog-catcher, constable and superintendent of snowfence,
it had a trout-killer. Like I was saying, the word predates Willie,
trout-killer being what fishermen were called in England about the
time of King John. Those remembering the legend of Robin Hood
will recall John was a nasty fellow. Trout killing, deer slaying, rabbit
snatchin', even gathering firewood had been illegal activities since
the Norman Conquest.

The English, not to miss a chance at spite when one abundantly
presented itself, have called themselves Anglo-Saxons ever since.
By all that is historically cogent, they should have been Anglo-
Normans; that they are not reflects on how the Normans didn't
make themselves very welcome. Not only were the French queer-
sounding, but they hogged the land, all of it: lock, stock and trout
pool. Wasn't a cooney or hind that wasn't preempted by the guys in
the big house. Not a partridge, pigeon or magpie.

If murder and theft received remonstration at the bailey, trout-killing got even worse. Hands were severed, eyes plucked, toes, feet, forearms, ears, lips severed. The curious thing is, not even this enthusiasm for law and order halted the behavior. One account tells of a poacher separated from his every natural appendage, only to be found dipping his line in the Earl's own salmon yard. In the end they hanged him, though were afraid to bury him in the kirkyard lest he somehow escape, so they buried him at sea. And as any fisher will testify to this day, English salmon disappear in the direction of the man's last known address.

An old custom it is then, in Yankee towns, to call a person a trout-killer, a venerable office in rural parts, same as the superintendent of snowfence is venerable. To tell of Willie the Trout-Killer is to speak also of the marsh, the Buena Vista Marsh, what locals amongst themselves call the Boney Vieux — a twisted voyageur expression meaning "old bone." How the place came to be called the Boney Vieux is not exactly pertinent to the story but since we're in no hurry you might as well know it.

❖

The central region of Wisconsin has been long and widely known as the Pinery, the terrain's intrinsic feature being its unremarkability. A plainer landscape would be hard to find without importing it. In the thousand million years since becoming dry land it had learned no vocation, sought no higher office and had been repeatedly glaciated, leaving behind a terrain composed of coarse, infertile soil.

The Buena Vista Marsh, called the moor by those wishing to sound polite and muck by those who don't, is the one precarious feature of this unenthusiastic landscape. A moor so flat, a convenient yet honest adjective is unavailable to describe it. If the neighboring earths are an admixture of bright sands laid down in gentle undulations, the Buena Vista has the appearance of a prostrate and well-chewed victim. The marsh, you see, had been chewed, same as a plug of Red Man is chewed, chewed, and rechewed, turning sour in the cheek of this awful place until it was spit out ten, twenty, thirty thousand years ago. Thousands of years of chew and spit beneath the glaciers and dab flat as ugly can get.

The meltwater of the ice had nowhere to run owing to the terrible flat, so for thousands of generations it was sphagnum moss, lichen, tamarack, willow, dogwood, cattails, sedge, alder, with the occasional popple thrown in. On the Boney Vieux a reluctant nature grew, turned sickly and died. Its offspring died the same; twenty thousand years of this living, dying, dropping dead in the still-cold water. Chew and spit, chew and spit.

Any undertaker can tell you cold is a better embalming agent than any chemical devised by modern science. No pumps, no formaldehyde, no pennies on the eyes. Everything that ever lived and died on the Boney Vieux got embalmed, chewed but never swallowed. The soil as a result had a queer and spongy behavior, was disagreeable of smell and black as a plug of confederate-issue. To the enterprising but gullible pioneer, the marsh looked like the grandest earth agriculture could hope for; not since Iowa had such raven-haired fertility been seen. Hundreds – make that thousands – of emigrants took up small holdings, the horizon dotted with their homes and outbuildings.

Soon after, it was evident the marsh lacked some vital element; crops thrived, then mysteriously lost their will and died. What didn't mysteriously die was killed by early frost – frost when there oughtn't be any, it being the middle of July. None imagined the moraine to the east of the marsh bore the place such ill will. Terrible summer nights when every chill, menacing molecule rolled off the moraine to stunt corn and wheat. The pioneers had no choice but to move on, less enthusiastic than when they arrived and much wiser. The hopeful little houses went unsold, fell into disrepair and joined the rest of the undead in the jealous earth of the Boney Vieux.

Other attempts to vitalize the marsh followed. An improvement company ditched the region and straightened out the tangled creeks, connecting a framework of canals described in illustrated brochures along with the great opportunity to get in on the ground floor. A small downpayment, low interest, housing available; barns also, some in need of repair. So they came again, lingered awhile and went away. The fields surrendered once more to tamarack and popple. Streams born under ice-dreamt hills yawned across the useless expanse, at least useless to the polytechnic who thought wheat was the only purpose of every land.

❖

Trout streams enjoy their immortality in a genteel fashion, though membership has its requirements. The Brule River, a hundred and ten miles north of Boney Vieux, has a gravel bottom; so do the Prairie and the Flume, the Tomorrow and the Little Wolf. They are trout streams of deserving legend. The implication is: any equal talent needs a gravel bottom since waders are quite useless if the creek bed doesn't hold the major length of the trouteer above water. Let a fisherman die in mire and rumor spreads like a speckled contagion that the ditch that done it is infected, quicksand maybe.

The Buena Vista didn't have quicksand but maybe a relative; in fact the speed of descent in muck is several times faster than quicksand. If it doesn't kill the fisher, the scare is enough to alter his mind. After a lesson or two in freefall, most participants put the Buena Vista at the bottom of their list of trout spas; besides, the water is too cold. Never mind what you've heard about trout water, even the worm apprentice knows water can get too cold for trout, since trout in cold water grow about as fast as the Joshua tree. If cold water and mucky bottom isn't disinclination enough, brook trout complete the curse. Any self-respecting trouteer must, for conscience, bypass brook trout since they don't get big enough to wallpaper a room and lack an essential enthusiasm for tied flies. A brown trout will bite at a dry fly if it annoys him, a rainbow does so out of jealousy; but if a brook trout isn't hungry, it isn't of a mind to go out to dinner, whether or not the nightclub has dancing girls.

❖

Willie farmed on the Main Road for most of six thousand years, least that's how people felt about Willie. He was that permanent, more a sandstone butte than a six-foot length of mortality. When he retired from farming he offered a spectacle rarely seen in agricultural precincts.

Farmers believe it is incumbent on them to die in harness and most plan for it, which doesn't do the resale value of the harness any favor. Willie ignored the code. He didn't want to die shoveling oats, since he had already died well and often enough doing chores. Never mind retiring isn't what farmers are supposed to do. You can talk retire all you want, but to actually sell off the cows, the brood sows and the corn right down to the last mouse nest is unpatriotic. Willie rented out his land, sold the tractors 'cept for a dyspeptic Farmall whose will to start coincided with the provident temperature to plant peas. No chickens, no sheep, no baling hay, no nothing that looked like it had a chore attached.

At this point everybody knew for certain Willie was gonna sell out the biggins and move to the village like any person should who is wise enough to have money in the bank. He didn't. What Willie did was infect the rest of the farmship with as bad a case of self-doubt as it ever had. On a hot summer morning a neighbor who had already broken down twice and was on his way to town for parts, had to drive by Willie's. Being on the Main Road, his place was unavoidable. Being one of those glued-together July mornings, only seven o'clock and already sweat was seeping through the shirt, hotter than sin even with the windows of the truck rolled down, overalls sticking to the legs and the day hardly started. Driving by Willie's place.

Mister Retired Farmer Willie. Willie wearing a flannel shirt in his boxelder-shaded kitchen, frying pancakes with bacon on the side. Had to drive the pickup through a ten foot high drift of bacon aromatics emanating from Willie's stove, one of those old-fashioned trash burners fired with corn cobs and shingles. Willie waving his coffee cup as he drove by feeling hotter than a steel mill rivet. Willie waving his la-de-da wave, wearing a November flannel shirt on this molten damnation of July. Showing off his retirement in the shade of his summer kitchen and a five course breakfast.

Mother of Jesus, there ain't nothing harder to take than a farmer in retirement, which is why it's better they move to town or die outright. Morally corrupting it is. Willie wasn't considered very kind 'cause he had neighbors doubting their calling and purpose in life. He had menfolk mad at themselves and the sun no more than two frecks off the horizon, not to mention how the scent of bacon sticks to the interior of a pickup, how out of self-preservation a farmer'd take the long way around to get to the hardware store, how even so they hit an eddy that smelled like Willie's bacon and this way the heck over on section 21 – wind currents or something.

❖

Willie took to trout same as a schoolboy falls in love with the first girl to wear lipstick. He fished the Boney Vieux from the week after trout season opened till it closed. He avoided the first week 'cause he didn't want to get trampled by the stampede of opening morning. Fishing through a forest of elbows and store-bought gear wasn't his idea of transcendental, neither were those fishing vests with the dainty wool pads. Neither were premium India-rubber waders costing more than a set of Montgomery Ward snowtires. Opening day fishermen wore hats without a high water mark; a man with a crisp hat is not honorable even when it is festooned with imitation insects. The first week was a regular bull fight out on the creeks, with more flourish and brush stroke than Pablo Picasso, whipping a fly through the air with aerobatics enough to upset a tree swallow's stomach.

Willie didn't care for the castigating look village fishers gave his eight-buckle galoshes nor his recycled fiberglass pole. His gear didn't have any breeding. Add to this offense, Willie didn't use flies. Didn't care for flies. Doubted flies. Reviled flies. Fly fishing was an abomination, what sort of man invented fly fishing in the first place? Fly fishing is contrary to the New Testament . . . when the Good Book asks the disciples to go forth and be fishers of men it expects them to dig decent bait, not some spangled, hood-winking bauble without food value. A fly fishing church is a lot closer to a whore-house or a french restaurant than a place of decent nourishment.

Willie was a worm man: red worms, grubs, maggots, night-crawlers. The closest he ever got to fly tying was a gray-beard grasshopper hooked through the thorax who lifts off the water a couple times before the policy is cashed. Give a trout an honest meal was Willie's attitude, matching the hatch makes no more sense than matching the washed bank for the recently drowned. Willie wasn't after philosopher fishes; philosopher fish are picky about their food, they will go hungry if the menu doesn't please them, they are connoisseurs and can afford it.

The way Willie saw it, if God had wanted men to fly fish he'd have used the split-bamboo approach himself. God wasn't interested in sport, he wanted trout to swallow the hook and take supper serious. What constitutes a good and fitting measure of trout is a frying pan. Suffer the little trout to come unto me, Willie said.

❖

Folks didn't mind the trout-killer. What they minded was his near ruin of agriculture. About first light on a spring morning he went by in that desiccated, four-door DeSoto of his, the pole protruding at a pornographic angle from the side window. If a farmer had missed Willie's previous definition of purgatory, this second installment got the meaning clear and they knew they were in it. That any decent person could rattle by at such an hour with no more care in the world than to pose in eight-buckle galoshes at the hem of a nameless stream to fish trout was criminal. Criminal . . . it was torture. A stab in the back, a poke in the eye, it was adultery, open air adultery and worse.

Farmers came to fear the sound of that DeSoto, the rattle of its undercarriage, they with a thousand chores to do, cows to milk. If a farmer wasn't contemptuous of trout at the outset he soon got that way.

Worse yet was when Willie went by about mid-afternoon to try another one of his secret places. A look to the pickle patch revealed it was empty except for the abandoned hoes leaning on the fence. The lot of 'em kidnapped for an hour's worth of Willie. Farmers there were who'd rather see their children attend a Sunday school taught by Joseph Stalin, thinking the Communist Manifesto wasn't near as corrosive to work habits as the ways of trout. Kids who might otherwise have grown into responsible adults became missionaries of trout. Once a kid learned what makes trout water, what causes a hole to be carpeted with brookies, he is no longer content to sit out the summer evening on the porch. He dreams of sandbags and pursed streams.

Willie took them, kid by kid, bairn by bairn, snatched them off the hayrack, nettled them from the potato patch. They disappeared from the pastures and the load of second crop didn't get put in the mow like it was supposed to. All a farmer heard was the brakeshoes grind, a door close and they were gone. An hour or two later a similar patent announced their return, having been someplace their father owned but never knew.

❖

A share of those kids became farmers, though less devoted than their fathers before, addicted from an early age, for they had seen the evening pool. The scene had captured them, caught in their marrow as they watched Willie bait a number eight brass with a mealworm the color of mahogany, a dab of lard for buoyancy. Turned on the current, the hook followed the stream where it went and disappeared in the undercut. A trout flopped after it and Willie gathered the line in wide loops till the winking fish was at his feet.

With a trout for breakfast he'd retire to the bank, cut a plug for his pipe and, not saying anything intelligible, clean the fish, wind the body in grass, put it in his pocket and walk back to the car. In the interval it had gotten dark.

Let a bird call and he knew it. Thrush, he'd say, whippoorwill, owl, catbird, heron; they following his sound back through the trees as he hadn't taken off his galoshes. Fearing they'd lose him, they learned his scent. Gaining the car, he put the coat in the trunk, stashed the pole, got in and kicked the starter. Sometimes he'd let one of them drive as far as their own place. Nobody said anything. No plans for another time. If they heard him coming and could make off without a father's notice they went, if not, then another time.

From May to September, a rainy afternoon was orphaned without the sound of the DeSoto. He'd stop, they impatient to get in before they were seen. He drove like an old man must – I don't think he ever used first gear – instead urging the DeSoto off in second, leaving it there when he ought have gone to third. He took the car down a logging road a pickup shouldn't try, branches scratching against the windows. A big limb caught underneath and took out the muffler, fence wire fixed it. Willie seemed oblivious to it all.

We'd walk in when the trail quit, sometimes down to ditch eight or hike up to Bannock's mill or the drought dam by Ostranders. Widow Ostrander, when she saw it was Willie, came out with a plate of sugar cookies. Willie took one, we ate the rest and Mrs. Ostrander sat on the bank holding the china plate, white as the moon in her hands. Willie coiled his line and let it out for another try. Nobody said anything, even to thank her for the cookies. Sometimes there were no trout.

He died in '72. The Missus sold off the farm and moved to Milwaukee to live with the son. The farmer who bought the place burned the buildings one summer afternoon. The volunteer fire department put it out and relit it half a dozen times before they finally let the house go. Intended to do the same with the barn but it got a draft they couldn't wet down.

Scattered around the township are a dozen kids who went off with Willie, farmers now – a thousand acres here, twelve hundred there, a shed full of John Deeres and a computer, two or three Harvestores. I've met them back in the marsh, parking my pickup next to theirs and walking to a pool we've known since . . . since . . .

We don't say anything, just swat mosquitoes and coil the line. Sometimes there's trout, sometimes not. Sometimes we find a kid to bring along and eat Oreos at the old drought dam, the moon bright as Chinese porcelain.

– *Jim Goetz*

Doug McLean grew up in a small Wisconsin village where, as a boy, he roamed the woods and fields that now appear as settings in his short stories. After education at the University of Wisconsin, he returned to Fond du Lac County to teach high school business and English for 36 years, then retired at age 59 to care for his disabled wife.

For recreation, McLean bowhunts for deer, searches for arrowheads and hikes and canoes with a camera or sketch pad close at hand. At his home, an old rural parsonage near Brownsville, he experiments with his newest hobby, writing.

McLean's stories, often published in the Wisconsin Outdoor Journal, emphasize the richness and beauty of nature and the outdoor experience, and illustrate the lessons about life that can be learned in the wilds. "The Ten-Year Deer," McLean's first outdoor story, is an example of his introspective style.

The Ten-Year Deer

by

Douglas McLean

Where was the buck, and how long before I would see him? If ever! The last sign I had seen of him was a quivering jackpine branch. My arrow had hit him; his flight had taken him over the fallen jackpine. After that, silence, stillness. It was as if the very pines and ferns were going to keep quiet about the event and testify that nothing had happened. But I wanted that buck, felt I deserved him, and I had waited a long time.

Deciding that I could wait a little longer, I sat on a limb up in the tree stand, with my thoughts. I knew that wanting was not going to work in this case, just as wanting my wife, Dorothy, to recover would never make it happen. I had left her at home with a sitter, as Huntington's Disease destroyed more of her brain cells. This was to be one of my last hunting trips as I took upon myself the increasing sacrifices of a caregiver, and, while I accepted the duty willingly, I often choked upon my inability to change or control events in my life. Now I stood gloomily in a tree, expecting that nothing would change the fact that the deer was gone for good.

Such thoughts could not totally dispel the good feeling that comes with Indian summer days at Meadow Valley Wildlife Area. There, free of charge and no appointment necessary, are whispering breezes in the jackpines, white birches against evergreens, the tawny, waving grasses, and, at night, the campfires, owl and coyote voices, and the wheeling canopy of icy-blue constellations.

Days like these should be embraced, indulged in fully, without guilt. Henry Thoreau said that he needed four hours a day in woods and fields to preserve his health and spirit. If we are denied the restorative power of a few such days, then the guilt should belong to those who deny.

When we had arrived in shirtsleeve weather the previous day, I had lain flat on my back for a time in the soft meadow grass and gazed up through the branches of an oak tree, a recommended first step in the restorative process. Then I had taken up my bow and walked a quarter mile back from camp, across a cutover area that was growing back to scrub oak and little jackpines. Faint summer deer trails crossed here and there.

Past the cutover, I followed a deer path into a woods, found a good climbing tree, and spent the remainder of the afternoon waiting twelve feet up, watching the path. Nothing happened, unless you count the peaceful notes of geese flying back to some flowage, or the two red squirrels that climbed my tree. Bits of bark fell on me as they scrambled up and down the trunk I was leaning against. Sometimes they stopped on a branch near my face for a look at me. If I had blinked an eye, there would have been an explosion of squirrels.

While waiting there, I recalled that east of my perch some distance there was the fieldstone foundation of a house, probably the site of a home of one of the farmers who lived here in the early 1900s. It is so deep in the woods that I needed a compass to relocate it on those occasions when I have returned, since first discovering it, while following up a missed grouse. The west and south side of the foundation are still visible there among the trees and ferns. The other sides have fallen into the basement, which is nearly full of humus and rock, with trees growing out of it.

I have gone there now and then to sit on the rocks and speculate about the farmer who once lived there. Did he build this place under lofty white pines, a few of which remain in the area, and listen to the play of breezes in their branches, or, on occasion, hear the rushing winds of storm? Did his kids romp in the woods, help in the fields, and ride in the farm wagon to town once a month? And where was his driveway? No sign of it now, or any clue to the rest of his life, either. Just these foundation stones I almost didn't see one day.

Where once there was a home with life pulsing strongly in times of joy, and weakly under illness or bad luck, now only grouse peck about the old foundation, and chickadees flit silently in the foliage above, leaving the observer to reflect on the impermanence of our efforts and the fragile duration of our good years.

While I had seen no deer from my tree, this was to be expected. We wait for years, enjoying the outdoors and companionship all the while, but always hoping that we will get a deer. At my level of participation the deer come about ten years apart, and lately I had begun to believe that time was running out; age and commitments were going to wreck the equation. Climbing trees and cliffs was becoming hard work, and free time was spoken for. To get a deer with bow and arrow, it's best to be young and strong and persistent, with time to burn.

Slowly then, the earth turned a few more degrees away from the sun, the dark trees merged with their darker shadows, and I was more than ready to leave the woods. Superior man, lover of sun-lit nature, finds there is a time to humbly hurry away from the night and give the woods back to its own. While I will not admit to looking furtively back over my shoulder, it seems that my sub-conscious contains inherited memories of sabre-toothed tigers and their cohabitants. This is when it is time to walk fast and look eagerly ahead for the light of the campfire. Ancient men must have also felt the pleasant anticipation of arriving back at that fire where the familiar silhouettes of fellow humans moved about, preparing for the evening food and fellowship.

Next morning I was back in the cutover again. While the sun found another glorious way to break through the clouds of daybreak, I sat on a log and took some pictures. It was a refreshing, beautiful place to be. Peace and vitality broke through the clouds of my spirit, and I felt no urge to be up and hunting.

Instead, I began to chuckle inwardly about what had happened the previous evening, a Saturday night. We had climbed down out of our trees at sundown and headed for the little town of Babcock, because two of our number were Catholic and wanted to attend Saturday night Mass. I and the other non-Catholic tagged along. When we stepped into that brightly lit rural church wearing our camo suits with camo paint on our faces, the service was already in progress, and many eyes turned toward us, increasing our embarrassment. Also, the pews were full, so we turned to a stairs leading to a rear choir loft, and upon reaching the top, we were motioned to some folding chairs by the organist and were handed choir hymn books; we were members of the choir! No choir robes, just camo hunting outfits, but we were willing.

Before our first number, however, we began to experience a new embarrassment. It had to do with the sermon the priest was giving. Just as we had gotten seated and tuned in to his voice, we heard him say, "and as for those who climb trees to look around . . ."

Oh, oh – he's going to lambaste the bowhunters, we thought, and scrunched down in our seats and hid behind our choir music.

Well, it turned out that it wasn't us he was talking about, but Zacchaeus, the man who climbed a tree for a better look at Jesus. It was a good sermon, too, and we relaxed. We knew we were in the clear when the priest handed us communion wafers on the way out.

We got no compliments on our singing, though.

A deer path ran past the log on which I sat, and, reluctantly, I got up to follow it. It led to the same woods I had been in yesterday. Eventually, I came to the same tree I had sat in then, but this time I was passing by on the other side of the tree. So two paths went by this tree, and I hadn't even noticed this one yesterday. Well, two paths made it worth another climb, even though it was already 7:30 a.m.; so up I went, and trimmed a few dead branches so that I could get a shooting angle at the new trail.

My back against the tree trunk, my feet placed to give me a shot at the new trail, I settled back. My bow and arrows hung on a branch in front of me. The morning sun shone through the colored feathers of the arrows with a pleasing effect, so I took out my camera to take a picture of the whole rig hanging there. I had hardly put the camera back and picked up the bow when one of my senses, difficult to say which, caused me to turn my head to the left to look at a movement. It was a deer, walking fast, toward me, along the new trail. I would have been late raising my bow had the deer not paused alertly about ten yards from my tree.

What a breathtaking creature, standing there! Motionless, but vibrant with life! Soft brown, yet radiant from the brush of creation. How easy it would have been, and possibly, how right, to have contracted buck fever at that moment and let the deer escape. But I had been practicing long the previous day, and so it was involuntarily that I raised the bow, drew, and released the arrow.

Deer never seem to fall over when hit, or sink to the ground like characters do in films. Hit fatally, or not hit at all, it seems the same: a panic leap and dash out of the area. Now, bright feathers that I had just photographed caught sunlight again as the deer carried my arrow in great leaps away from the trail. Another moment and the deer collided with a bush. A slight stumble and it was away again, leaping over a fallen jackpine.

The deer was gone. Needles of the jackpine vibrated from its passage. Another deer had performed the vanishing act, the disappearance which can take place even when your eyes never waver from the animal. Such is the superb blending of deer with forest, and the silent smoothness of their movements. This deer was probably now gliding quietly through marsh grass and cattails into some impenetrable swamp, and I would have trouble following. I was also concerned about my hit; it seemed to have been weak and possibly not well placed.

While I waited the usual twenty minutes, the sun came up fully and promised a balmy day. While chickadees flitted and squirrels rustled in the leaves, negative thoughts about a poor hit and hard tracking gave way to more positive ones. After all, the deer was hit and might lie down nearby, and I would not be tracking it in bad weather or in the dark. From my perch, I took a few more photos. Would there be a photo of that deer later today?

I took out my small binoculars and scanned the general area where the deer had run, and then my heart sank. There was my arrow lying on the ground, twenty yards away, a certain sign of poor penetration. Finally, I lowered my bow on a cord and climbed down after it, then walked over to the arrow, and the outlook immediately improved. It was only half an arrow. Broken off, the front half remained with the deer.

I continued on past the place where the deer had ricocheted off the bush, and on to the jackpine deadfall. This tree, a recent storm victim, still had its needles. The tip of the tree pointed towards me. I moved along the left side toward its base and the marsh beyond. I dreaded trying to follow that deer through the water. I've seen how easily deer can splash through these areas, even when they are breaking through thin ice. Beneath the tree, a small patch of something like birch bark was visible. What duels the mind has with itself! Consciously, I wanted to ignore this trivial distraction, get past the tree, and look for a blood trail into the marsh.

"Get going, you wishful thinker; that is nothing worth checking out," said one part of my brain. Another part formed no words, just turned my feet around and marched me toward investigation. I hurried back around the tip of the tree and came up the right side for a better look. As I came even with where I had been on the other side, I began involuntarily to slow, and all the while the dueling in my head was still going on, with a third speaker entering to tell the dueling parts to shut up and feel the excitement building.

The fallen jackpine was dense and eight feet thick at this point. I was now even with the white spot. I stopped. There was nothing there. Stepped forward. Parted some branches. There, like a hidden fawn, deep in this bushy tree, lay a fat buck, white belly fur blazing up through the needles. What relief! What satisfaction! I walked up slowly and gently tugged his ear. He was dead, all right, and I was experiencing an emotion that even early man must have felt, a bittersweet mixture of elation and sadness. One can understand why Indians paid respect to the spirits of the animals they killed.

After the buck was tagged, there was time to reconstruct the events. When the deer had bounded away from the trail and hit a bush at twenty yards, I took the collision to be from blind panic, but, apparently, the deer was already weakening. When he recovered his balance and headed for the deadfall, my view was partly blocked. I could not see beyond the deadfall, where his leap would have taken him, so I assumed he had completed his leap, especially with that jackpine twig vibrating mockingly. But it had not been so. Instead of clearing it, heart failing, he had struck the branches and fallen back into that little nest where I found him; the last leap of his life.

Half an hour later we had him back in camp. That evening around our deep-woods campfire we enjoyed baked potatoes and deer tenderloins. Later, as I reclined by the fire and studied the embers, my satisfaction wasn't just with the deer alone. It seemed I had gained something more, something connected to that old fieldstone foundation and those who had lived there. If the stones back in that shadowy, moonlit grove could speak, they might tell of a family that was happy in spite of things beyond their control. Life held very few guarantees in those days, and those folks probably had learned a lesson I was just beginning to understand, that sufficient joy can be found in small ways at infrequent times, that anticipation of these moments can sustain us, and experiencing them can renew us.

The ten-year wait was over, and I had gotten a bonus. While oak leaves whispered above and night mists settled on the meadow beyond, I crawled into my sleeping bag, believing that, for me, these days at Meadow Valley were only the beginning of a new appreciation of life. 🍂

— Sharon Anderson

Born in Waukesha and raised in Genesee, Dick Yatzeck is Professor of Russian Literature at Lawrence University in Appleton. He lives near Bear Creek and the Wolf River, where the ruffed grouse and walleyes find it easy to elude him.

When not teaching or in the woods he enjoys walks with his wife, Diane, on Blueberry Road, listening to his daughter Sarah's saxophone, and reading The Yearling or Treasure Island to his son David at bed time, as he once read them to his older daughters, Elena and Tanya, now gone out into the world.

Yatzeck lectures on Russian, and sometimes German, English and American literature. These lectures, he says, "can be boring, but are invariably high-minded." He believes, with Pasternak, that reading is the highest human activity but ought to be done "as unpretentiously as cleaning potatoes or carrying water." His students don't always agree. Why should they? They need to find their own joy.

Turgenev's Sportsman's Sketches and Faulkner's The Bear are Yatzeck's models, though he admits his own writing "has never come anywhere near them." His stories have appeared in The Turkey Hunter, Gray's Sporting Journal, and Wisconsin Outdoor Journal.

Strong Brown God
by
Richard Yatzeck

"I think that the river is a strong brown god . . . implacable."

–T. S. Eliot

Curry and I are fishing the Wolf north of one of the little river towns in the central part of the state. Late March, the walleye run. I swear, every year the *Post Crescent* runs the same picture of a grizzled local and his feral wife holding up a string of five-pound walleyes. Same three-day, pepper-and-salt beard on him, same quick blank eyes on her, same dented aluminum jon boat. And Curry and I rise out of a perfectly comfortable faculty office to this frowsy, battered bait.

There's snow on the barren banks, the wind cuts like a dull splitting maul, and the metal boat seat raises hemorrhoids like boils. Ice forms in the guides, minnows freeze almost as fast as fingers, and narrow pans of ice threaten to sweep us right off the brown water. But we come – happily, ecstatically – to be skunked. Three years, five years running.

This day doesn't seem appreciably different. After six windy hours the coffee's gone, the sandwiches are sodden, Curry's eaten both cans of sardines and the spare paddle, and we've caught a rock bass that looked as if it had been swallowed and spit out by a northern. And two smallish mudpuppies. Actually, that's better than usual.

It's almost four. We've anchored and floated almost down to town and the second car when my reel handle does a slow turn against the too-tight drag. The line must be out seventy-five yards. I've been sagging against the gunwale, eyes half shut, meditating about the attack of three horny drake mallards on a half-drowned hen, and it takes a while to react. Still, I reel in slack, point the rod out of the boat and upstream toward the west bank, and haul back smartly enough. Whatever's there feels like a soggy barstool cushion. I smack it again.

Curry: "You got a fish?"

Me: "Something. Feels like I'm snagged on a deer carcass."

But I reel, Curry rows, and a thick, mottled back duly appears next to the now trembling net. Swish-plop, swish-plop and, by the grace of a for-once careless Wolf River, we have a six-and-one-quarter-pound walleye in the net, in the boat, and after a good long untangling time, on a clip stringer. The first real fish for either of us in five years of spring runs. The first walleye over two pounds that either of us has seen close up. Adrenaline flows as we drift into the river hamlet.

"Let's celebrate that one with a beer and a sandwich," says Curry, an economist who usually knows the difference between sport and the bottom line. We tie up under the town's ancient metal bridge. I play nonchalant, but tie the stringer to the propeller, then sink the whole business far out of sight behind the boat. We can watch the boat from the bar.

Freddy's River Tap. Gravy-brown woodwork, smell of pee and stale tap beer – pretty much the same smell. Hotdogs and Tombstone pizzas on the menu, so we order two of each, two snowshoes, and two bottles of Bud. A quick look out the window shows the boat unmolested. It's starting to snow on the dark water.

Besides us and the slight, stooped bartender there are three locals and a girl in a buckskin vest at Freddy's. It's the late seventies and country-looking girls have begun to occur even here. Soon we're eating pizza, I'm watching the boat, and the three locals, just in from the day shift at the veneer mill, have tried the shake off the day and are studying what looks like a pile of photographs. The girl downs a shot of bar brandy. Kind of like a man, convulsively. Freddy's has one of those pro-feminist posters of a girl in jeans crowded between two wondering guys at a trio of urinals, but this girl doesn't even glance at it.

Curry suggests that the locals are studying French postcards, "feelthy peektures," but the bartender just says "gummint fish." The Wolf is the main spawning territory of lake sturgeon, the only open season is a two-week spearing possibility on Lake Winnebago, with odds rather worse than Las Vegas. These are photographs of the sturgeon poached last May, against the rather daunting threat of innumerable wardens and thousand-dollar fines.

"You guys do any good?" asks the nearest local, the one in the Jacques Seedcorn cap.

"Naw . . . mudpuppies," answers Curry, who has learned how unfashionable the truth is in such situations. The girl at the other end of the bar belts another brandy and pulls her ten-gallon over her eyes. Curry orders another Tombstone.

The fish in the photographs are large – the fishermen in the pictures don't hold them toward the camera; they struggle to support them on what look like Navy-issue hawsers. In the river town, which is only formally governed out of Madison, the rite of passage is the capture of an illegal sturgeon, against whatever odds. In the thirties there was a lucrative trade in sturgeon, roe, and walleyes. Many a family stayed off of relief by poaching. Now some of the young men risk cars, licenses, and hefty fines to rival their fathers and grandfathers. Still, it's become largely an expensive game. It's no longer necessary.

The girl gets up and goes over to the juke box. She puts in six quarters and makes her selections. She comes back to the bar to inhale another brandy. She takes off her scanty vest. "Good looker. Half-Indian. She's from Bear Creek," says the bartender. Three or four other locals have arrived as she ascends a sort of drum-shaped dais in the back corner of the small dance floor across from the bar. A today-ancient ancestor of rock paces the gyrations of her brown young body, of her short, fringed leather skirt. She keeps her eyes closed; the brandy hasn't helped much.

And nobody but the bartender, Curry and I, looks. Nobody. The locals, latecomers and regular afternooners, are deep in the study of sturgeon. The girl's dancing is halting. Her body is firm and young. She wishes she were dead – or, at least, not quite so broke. But no one notices, except us.

"Curry," I say, "I have to get out of here." Curry's from Chicago and finds the act awkward, but not especially offensive. Still, he sees my sympathetic discomfort and pulls on his parka with no fuss. He even leaves half of his third pizza on the bar. Exit.

Back at the boat I heave up the motor, look miserably at the walleye, then unclip the stringer and drop the fish convulsively in the river. It flexes once and is gone.

"What the . . .?" inquires Curry.

"They didn't even notice her," I answer. "I won't fish in the same river with the bastards!"

"Oh," says Curry, "that's all right, then." As I said, he knows the bottom line, usually.

Then we go to get the other car and the trailer, come back to town for the boat, and head home. The Wolf wasn't careless after all.

❧

– *Paul Birling*

Timothy L. Personius grew up on the edge of the Horicon Marsh in south central Wisconsin, the setting for his story, "A Lifetime of Chances." He developed a keen appreciation for the outdoors from his father, who managed the Horicon National Wildlife Refuge from the mid-1960s to the mid-1970s.

Today, Personius lives in Billings, Montana, with his wife, Nita, and his sons Ross and Robert. He works as an environmental specialist for the U.S. Department of the Interior's Bureau of Reclamation.

In his spare time, he writes an outdoor column for Fish Tales, *a statewide magazine, and tries to "stay out of the house as much as possible." That means trout and walleye fishing, hunting upland game birds, and pursuing elk in the Centennial Mountains of South Central Montana.*

A Lifetime of Chances
by
Timothy L. Personius

I remember certain fall days. The first fall days, really, when an uncertain cold front would drop out of Canada, temporarily pushing the muggy air of summer out of the upper Midwest. If you've ever lived there, you know how refreshing those suddenly clear, brisk days can be – days when you want to live just to breathe that clear, cool air from the tundra.

Those fronts also brought thousands of geese to my home in Wisconsin, on the edge of Horicon Marsh. Canada geese – big, black, white and gray. I'd hear the murmuring rumor of them for some days; a late night whisper of honking, far away in the dark. I'd look for them every morning, sometimes calling my father at the federal wildlife refuge headquarters to ask if anyone had yet seen them.

Finally they'd arrive – chevron after chevron traced thinly against the sky, looming larger in their descent – some nearly overshooting the refuge and resorting to a spectacular side-slip stall, plummeting like skydivers until they unfurled their wings with a rifle-sharp crack of suddenly compressed air. For a moment, even now, the air is filled with the snapping reports of braking geese, and I am standing outside our house, watching them settle softly over the marsh. In my commonest memory, they arrive all at once, changing summer into fall, instantly, by their presence.

The geese were a package deal. You had to take the good with the bad. The good parts were many, and wonderful, and I don't know that I've ever been as content as when they sang me to sleep on crisp autumn nights. But later on, after the start of the hunting season, there was the bad part too – the cripples. They were the result, largely, of the slobs we collectively referred to as "Milwaukee hunters." In all fairness I cannot condemn every hunter from Milwaukee or Madison or Chicago that came to the marsh. But there was the certain sect of mostly suburban idiots who migrated to the marsh in the fall with the geese. The kind of "sportsmen" who measure the quality of their hunt by the number of rounds they fire.

To be sure, every hunter will at some time cripple and lose game. It is the inevitable consequence of pursuit. But there is a question of ethics, too, and another of competence. I was then, and I still am, a hunter. And I resist anyone's attempt to classify me in a group that includes them.

I think of the man I once saw kill a goose cleanly on his first shot and who was then ridiculed by his partners for having to end his "shooting" for the year – the limit on geese being one bird per season. On another occasion a pair of clowns came equipped with a super-8 movie camera. One filmed as the other shot a goose and then laughingly ran down the wounded bird and finished it off. The "hunter" swung the goose around in great circles by its head until, to his great amusement, the neck broke and tore away. The grinning sport was left holding up the bloody head for the camera.

But mostly the flock of cripples grew out of a practice known as "skybusting," exercised by those who didn't know the effective range of their weapons, or didn't care. This type of behavior was exemplified by a man I once observed from my own front porch, who crippled and sailed a dozen birds before he luckily broke the next bird's wing and was forced to collect it and quit for the day. He must also have been relieved, I think, to get away from our house and my redoubtable sister, who had charged him at least twice in his nearby blind, hurling insults and curses that surprised my mother and impressed me, at least, with their worldliness.

There was nothing I could do about the hunters. They came and went in their fat, shiny cars. They left behind a legacy of wounded geese. But there was something I could do about those birds.

On a typical fall day, the school bus would drop me off at the end of our driveway in the late afternoon. I can still feel the sense of relief I had when I finally jumped out of that stale, creaking bus, done with school for another day. Almost done, that is. I had one more thing to do.

I fairly ran down the half-mile-long dirt road to the old red-and-white farmhouse at its end, just inside the refuge boundary on the edge of the marsh. I was inside for only a minute, long enough to shuck off my stiff school clothes and pull on my faded and threadbare jeans, plaid shirt, patched rubber boots, a tattered camouflage jacket and a drooping canvas hat. Marsh clothes. Only then did I feel really finished with school and free from all the loathesome rituals that went with it.

I'd duck into the shed and stuff several small gunny sacks into the game pouch of my coat and then head across the old, overgrown cow pasture to the big fields of corn and alfalfa, also inside the refuge, that always harbored big flocks of loafing geese. I'd be excited and hopeful that today might be a good day, that I would find some of the cripples hiding in the great flocks, catch them, and take them home to join the sick and injured geese I had already captured.

In season, the makeshift pen in back of our long shed sheltered afflicted birds of many kinds: a great-horned owl, screech owls, ducks, pheasants, a rare swan, one great blue heron, a red-tailed hawk. And, of course, the geese. In my best season – not theirs – I caught 96 wounded geese, scratching the tally marks into the plaster wall outside the pen.

We sent most of these to game farms or zoos in the late fall, when there were no more to find. But others would die of their wounds, and a lucky few, those with wings broken beyond the outer joint, would heal well enough to fly again. There were very good and hopeful days when I would let these few out of the pen, cross my fingers for them, yell wildly, and chase them into the sky.

But catching the birds in the big fields had its moments, too. I would creep through the still-standing corn to mid-field, then crawl on my belly to the edge of the adjacent hay field where the birds usually rested in the late afternoon. By moving slowly on all fours, staying just inside the shield of screening corn, I was often able to crawl within twenty feet of the edge of a flock that numbered easily in the thousands. I sometimes stayed hidden for an hour or more, watching them graze and preen and squabble, laughing quietly at such a picture of organized confusion.

Sometimes I'd imagine a far away teacher shaking a concerned finger at me, scolding, "You should be more involved in extra-curricular activities." I laughed too loud at that thought once and the nearest geese looked my way with blinking concern. But I stayed silent and still for a while, and the geese forgot about me.

When the sun began to set behind me, I knew I'd have to make my move. Gathering my legs under me, I'd charge full bore into the open field, running all out just for the fun of it, crazily, yelling, laughing. Instantly, panic would spread through the flock. I'd be engulfed in a dark cloud of rising geese, deafened by the wild crescendo of thousands of pairs of pumping wings and a thousand-part honking harmony as the huge birds panicked all around and above me. Some crashed into each other in their mid-air hysteria –

Thwock . . . Thwock . . . Thwock – wings flailing wings as they scrambled into flight.

The geese disappeared rapidly. Most settled out on the marsh where they always roosted at night anyway. Some dropped into nearby fields for a last bite. I hope they didn't mind my intrusion too much. After all, I was there for a reason. I was there to find the handful of birds that could not join the others in flight, and I would run several lengths of that field each evening, chasing down cripples.

A Canada goose is a large bird, and when cornered it can present to the novice a sobering spectacle – feathers ruffled, hissing madly, wings held at the ready to batter the enemy with their club-like, thickened joints. Most of the cripples could be run down easily and pinned, the birds falling into a helpless, shock-induced stupor. Some were not so easy. Just as I was closing in on them, they would turn to confront me, holding their ground. Fewer still would actually attack. After one of these surprise counterattacks, and a rather embarrassing retreat on my part, I devised an effective capture technique for the bold ones.

Mimicking a snake charmer, I would entice them to strike at one of my hands with their bill. Then quickly grabbing their neck with my other hand, I would flip them on their back and pin them. This often worked. Other times, I would learn how sharply geese could bite. In either case, I eventually pinned the bird. Then, out came a gunny sack large enough to fit over the bird but snug enough to pin its wings. I tied the bag loosely around the base of its neck, so it couldn't worm out of captivity, then left it to run after the next cripple. When there were no more to be found, I would go back and collect the bagged birds, walking home through the then-silent fields, clutching two or three or even four lumpy, squirming bundles, a long-necked head of a bewildered goose protruding from each.

The new birds settled into the pen flock quickly, their size and fierceness determining each one's new rank in the pecking order, and they quickly adapted to my routine of caring for them. As the hunting season progressed, the flock grew larger and the days grew shorter. Eventually, it was dark when I fed them in the morning before walking down to meet the school bus.

The water tub would often freeze over, and I'd smash the crust with an axe and bring a bucket of hot water from the kitchen so that the geese might have longer to drink. It was harder to find any greenery for them in late fall, and later, when the snows came, I would pry up the weathered boards of an old pen to find a few handfuls of clover. The geese treasured these morsels most, disdaining any corn until the last green leaf was gone, squabbling and pecking for the last bite.

All the while, it never seemed like work to me. While I could be hard to find when the lawn needed mowing or the trash begged for burning, I never forgot to care for my birds. My birds. My special friends that I fed and watered and talked to and listened to and just liked to be around.

I liked to walk down the long narrow shed in the gloom of morning, more feeling than seeing my way, smelling the stack of bedding straw outside the pen and listening to the quiet clucks and cackles and whistles of the flock. Finally, the door would creak open at my touch, and the birds hushed instantly, shuffling to the far side of the pen. Uncertain. When steaming water splashed into the tub and rustling ears of corn dropped at their feet, they remembered and would scatter again, drinking, eating, squabbling, chattering, oblivious to the boy sitting quietly on the bale of hay in the corner. They pecked even at the corn the boy always left between his feet. Did they even see me? Did they know they were with a silent, smiling boy who suddenly felt too good to go to school and wondered if anyone would notice if he didn't?

I like to remember those mornings. Those were rare times for me, when getting up early was easy and the purpose rewarding. After we shipped the birds to the game farm, things were different. I avoided the shed for weeks. And mornings, bleak and still, were best slept through.

During the second year of my goose collecting, I started the mercy killings. By then, I'd seen enough birds die to recognize the doomed ones – the ones infected and poisoned with lead. I was already a surgeon of the crudest sort and had amputated several wings. That in itself was a difficult job. We operated only on birds with shattered wings, the ones with shards of bone jutting out. They would never fly again, and they seemed to wonder what the useless and stinking mass of feathers was that they constantly tripped on. So we would cut off the wing. One of my brothers or me holding the bird down, the other cutting quickly with a clean, carefully honed jackknife.

Sometimes it was easy . . . on us. And sometimes not. A severed blood vessel would suddenly squirt out a thin, curving stream of blood that splattered our clothes and hands. Then we had to pinch the twitching stub with our fingers until the flow stopped and the blood congealed and it was safe to let the stunned bird go. They plodded dazedly back to the flock, leaning crazily to one side until they learned to adjust to their lost symmetry. We plodded sullenly back to the house to wash off the blood. It was a funny feeling when a live bird's blood spurted all over your hands. Afterward, Mom made us wash up thoroughly, but for days I still felt the sensation of hot blood running down my fingers. It took me a long time to rub it away. I really don't know if we saved any geese with our surgery, but in spite of our crudeness, we never lost any.

Of course, the mercy killings were different. One morning I would open the door to the pen and, as the birds shuffled to the other side, one or two would be left behind, unable to walk. For a few days, their only locomotion was their wings; they'd push and flap themselves around to eat and drink. These birds, like the amputees, had to become fierce to maintain their rank and fill their crops. Eventually, their wings would fail too, and I would have to bring them their own corn and water, standing guard over them to make sure they had their fill. For them, however, the pattern was inescapable.

First the legs would go, then the wings, and ultimately the will. Their poisoned, infected bodies finally succumbed to a creeping paralysis. On their last day they would sit alone, neck drooping, head bobbing rhythmically up and down, milky eyes swollen nearly shut, gasping. In the mornings I would find their stiff, lonely corpses. Unable to bury them in the now-frozen ground, I would carry them down to the edge of the marsh, hurling them as far as I could. I watched with stony silence till the reeds unbent and resumed a swaying guard over their new charges. I'd trudge back up the hill to our house without looking back.

Too many died that way. I had this notion of cruelty then, and I thought that theirs was a cruel death. I didn't want to see it again. So I started to kill them.

I would wait till they couldn't move anymore, wait until I was sure they couldn't come back. I hoped every morning to see them back on their feet again. It never happened.

The first one was the worst. I watched the slow sickness taking over a large, fierce gander. I tried not to believe that he was doomed, but even his great will was not enough. I fed him separately for a couple days, trying not to look right at him, trying not to see his death approaching, slowly, inexorably. I don't know today if I wanted to kill him for my sake or his.

They had become my special friends, these birds. I couldn't save them, but maybe I could spare them. I debated how to do this. Should I shoot the gander, suffocate him, or even have a vet euthanize it for me? Eventually, I knew I couldn't have a stranger do it, that it was my obligation, a sorrowful portion of the commitment I had made to the geese, including this perishing gander, and that I would have to do it quickly and quietly.

I found a stout, short-handled club, ridiculously large for the task. I was going to do it in the morning, but I found many excuses to put it off till later. That evening, I could delay no longer. I walked into the pen and hoped he was already dead. The other geese bunched nervously in one corner, and he was left alone with me in another. He couldn't move around anymore, and he was starving slowly, unable to eat, or not caring to.

I knelt down beside him and sat still for some time. I wanted a miracle. I wished for one. I prayed for one.

"Show a little mercy, God . . . is that too much to ask?" I guess it was. I thought about the local priest who told me that the "other" animals didn't have souls, and don't worry about them. Just who the hell was he to know that? I was mad and scared and sad for the whole world and me and a goose.

I weakly raised the club above my head, summoning, it seemed, all of my strength to hold it there. Trying to comfort the gander and not knowing how, I cradled his sagging head in my free hand and felt a muffled, guttural honk work up his long neck, but the once-vibrant, resonating call vented quietly as a gasp. His milky eyes were seeing something else, far away from where we were.

For one last moment he was high, so very high, the half-frozen tundra far below and he was heading north, leading the flock, wings pumping, heart pounding, singing. And in a terrible moment, I suddenly knew every word to his song and heard every voice in the flock's clarion harmony. I looked to him for help, but he was gone. I saw that he had died weeks before, falling to earth, falling from grace. And before I could cry for him, the club arced resolutely down. He shivered a moment and then stilled. His life passed quickly, quietly.

There is, I think, some part within us that tries to save us from pain, covering and protecting us with a blanket of numbness. A kind of mental paralysis stops us from asking the endless, unanswerable questions, stops guilt and fear from taking over. The numbness came when I clubbed the goose to death. I was almost outside myself then, watching a grim little boy do this thing for me so I wouldn't have to feel it. Well, not much.

There were others after him, but none so difficult. I slowly acquired the traits of the man that destroy the boy. Stoicism. Cynicism. I don't think I was born a cynic. I remember endless hope and constant expectation, but no cynicism. I think my other faults – the greed, the jealousy, the capacity for hate – were always there, but the cynicism I had to grow and nurture myself. The hope got bashed in too often, the expectation always went unanswered. The geese died. They would never fly again. I began to kill the hopeless ones. Cynicism strengthened in me. I learned to see the gray in black-and-white.

I remember the high hopes I had in the beginning, in the first year, and I remember the weary resignation I had the last year. Finally I quit. I avoided the fields in the fall, where I knew I would find cripples. It was all hopeless.

I remember the day I lost the last goose. It was December. The marsh was freshly frozen over, the geese gone south. The ice was just solid enough to walk on, so I headed out among the cattails and muskrat houses for one last roundup of stray cripples. I shuffled along the slick, thin ice, half-stepping and sliding, listening to the sonorous ping and groan of settling ice and watching fresh cracks slice outward under my heavy boots. At last, the narrow channel I was following widened, opening into what we called the big ponds – a series of connected small lakes, really – and now a vast, gleaming shelf of ice, windswept clean of snow.

Across this shimmering expanse, a weak sun stealing away silently behind him, stood the last goose. His broken wing dangled limply on the ice and I could see that he was looking to the sky. Across the gulf of space between us the wind carried his thin, wavering call.

I could not catch this last goose. He outran me easily on the slick footing and disappeared into the snowless, encircling tangle of cattails, leaving a trail only a fox could follow . . . and would. And I, bent against the wind, turned my back once more, and shuffled my way home across a sea of singing ice.

It's hard to describe how you become so attached to a place where you worked and played, lived and took life, and loved and hated everything around you at one time or another. A place on which you look back and want to feel that you made a difference in. A farmer I knew put it this way: "You got to make your mark on the land. The most turrible thing in this life will be havin' to die without makin' your mark . . . knowin' you ain't left someplace no better'n you found it."

So I now look back at that place I hold so dearly and wonder if my 'mark' is there or not, knowing that I am forever marked by the marsh. It's hard to describe how I became so attached to it. Part of my fiber is part of its fiber. When I left it, I left behind some part of myself. My family moved away from the marsh when I was seventeen. It hurt: a dull ache – real, physical pain – deep inside.

One March, I was returning to my new home in Montana from a trip to the South. A scheduling conflict unexpectedly found me on a jet flying over central Wisconsin. We flew out of the megalopolis of the Milwaukee area and into the hinterlands of dairy country. It was late evening, but the lights from closely packed farms and small, ubiquitous towns, were visible everywhere below. Even at 20,000 feet the land was noticeably lighted. I peered out the tiny window, straining to see my old home, wondering if I would be able to recognize it from the air, suddenly realizing that I wouldn't need to. There was the marsh, plain as the night – a broad, oblong, black hole on the landscape. Thirty thousand acres of darkness, to be exact. My place. It hurt a little to fly over and not be stopping.

We crossed the marsh quickly, the dull ache again in my stomach and a thousand memories racing so fast I couldn't pick out a single one to stop the flow. All of them compressed into a sort of melody, the countless notes indiscernible. For me, it was the song of a home that I couldn't have again, a siren's song I heard but could not heed. Belted immobile in the jetliner, hurtling forward, I understood the torment of Odysseus, lashed to the mast of his ship.

And then, sometime later, I am huddled down behind a clump of willows along the Beaverhead River in southwestern Montana, hunting ducks. A flock of geese sounds in the distance and heads my way. Instinctively, I slip off the safety of my gun. Then I'm laughing to myself and pushing the safety back on.

The birds, about twenty, are coming right at me. When they are almost overhead I leap up and shout at them, "Too low, dummies!" Then, just talking, "Any fool could have had you." The flock splits around me and frantically gains altitude.

My hunting companion runs over to me, asking breathlessly if my gun was jammed and why didn't I shoot? I told him that I didn't shoot geese, as I had told him before. But he didn't believe me. After all, I had a license. "And the season's open! How could you miss a chance like that?"

How, indeed. How could I explain to him that I had already used up a lifetime of chances?

❧

– Paul Birling

From his home in Baileys Harbor, Tom Davis works as senior editor for Wisconsin Trails *magazine, contributing editor and gun dogs columnist for* Sporting Classics, *and as executive director of the Door County Land Trustees, a non-profit conservation organization. Davis also contributes to a variety of publications on a freelance basis. Although he travels widely to hunt and fish, perhaps his favorite sporting pursuit is gunning grouse and woodcock over his own pointers and English setters — in Peshtigo country.*

In Peshtigo Country
by
Tom Davis

We knew our destination by name only. It was a campground deep in the northern Wisconsin forest. According to the literature supplied by the Forest Service, a network of hunter walking trails, seeded to clover and closed to vehicles, lay nearby, across the Peshtigo River. Peshtigo: whatever it meant, the sound of it was irresistibly romantic. We imagined a country seething with grouse and woodcock, a land of unbroken timber inhabited only by the spirits of voyageurs and lumberjacks.

Other than a few books, records, and articles of clothing, I carried my worldly belongings with me: three English setters, two shotguns, a good fly rod, camera gear, camping equipment, and related paraphernalia. If anything, Adrian's material worth was less than mine. I owned the white-over-rust pickup, too, not in much better shape than it was when I sold it two years later for $150, cap included. The speedometer was the single gauge that worked. Because the gas gauge didn't, and because the tank was known to leak, we gave our business in tiny increments to numerous filling stations, just to be safe.

We topped it off in Wabeno, left the highway, and struck out

over the backroads. The moon had not yet risen. Our world compressed to the cone of vision defined by the headlights. We worried
the map like a pair of terriers, as if we believed it was holding out,
not telling us all that it could.

Then, out of the blackness, a sign appeared. We followed its
arrow into the deserted campground. As we approached site number
5, the moon emerged, spilling platinum across the lake. The water
bore its precious weight, a necklace across the breast of a dark-
skinned woman. The headlights limned a neat stack of split wood
standing next to the fire pit; we assumed this was Forest Service
s.o.p., only to discover later it was the largesse of the previous
occupants.

A flock of geese beat skyward as we stepped from the truck. We
fancied we could see them moving against the stars — we couldn't,
really — and their music filled the night, crowding out the sound of
our own breathing. As if in response, a pack of coyotes began
howling somewhere to the north, songs rising from those tilted
muzzles like messages aimed at space, but only us to hear them. The
Coleman lantern flared, then steadied. Adrian built a fire. We
washed cheese-and-onion sandwiches down with Hamm's beer, and
watched the sparks ascend and vanish.

That was our introduction to Peshtigo Country. Strictly by the
calendar, it wasn't that long ago. To Adrian and myself, hunting
grouse and woodcock there has come to seem like something we've
done forever, the intersection at which our lives have been aimed
since I was a kid skipping school to chase pheasants in Iowa, and
Ade was a lad in the west of England, casting nets for hake and
plaice into the Irish Sea. We've exchanged the impoverished
freedom of unemployment for the encumbered security of regular
paychecks, but we manage, every October, to return.

There is no single reason why. We return for the birds: for the
secretive woodcock, birds whose presence might never be revealed
save for the miraculous nose of a setter, birds that appear and

disappear as quickly and magically as the gold in the leaves of an aspen; for the grouse, maddening and adored, birds that almost combust with life, as if all the energy of the forest were somehow channelled into their beings. We return for the coverts, for the memories we've cached of points and shots, for the promises they keep and the ones they break.

We return for the fragments that compost camp life: the split-body sensation of being toasted on one side by the fire, and frozen on the other by twenty-degree air; the comforting, gaseous hiss of the Coleman; the sight of Zack, an old bear of a setter, ritualistically wetting down every bush within a fifty-foot radius of the tent; the delicious agony in shedding the cocoon-like warmth of a sleeping bag to face the frigid morning; Ade finding his contact lenses frozen in their solution; wolfing eggs and sausage as fast as the heavy skillet can fry them; brewing tea in a cold rain, cupping our numb hands around the mugs; watching the sun burn the mists off the lake.

And we return simply for the feel of this wild and lonely country. It is like a coat slipped over our shoulders when we're not looking: suddenly, it is just there. It is hidden in those endless timbered ridges, in those valleys dense with shadows, in the cool air that collects in the swamps. It is in the murmur of the alder-canopied creeks, the clean-edged track of a white-tailed buck, in the pure, brilliant sky. Mysterious, arterial, the Peshtigo is a presence at the heart of it all, the key to the soul of the country.

If the fabric of hunting the Peshtigo remains the same, its texture changes from year-to-year. The first trip was marked by revelations, both personal and objective in nature. Objectively, we discovered that a lot of the designated hunter walking trails wind through birdless, mature forest, but that there are still miles and miles of trails that penetrate likely cover. Personally, I discovered that, in an expansive outdoor setting, it is easy to confuse intoxication with euphoria. Ade and I started the cocktail hour with beer, then switched to Dewars after supper. When the Dewars ran out, we switched back to beer. We philosophized by the fire, devouring Snickers bars at a terrific rate, and generally felt . . . well, euphoric. This is all so great, we kept telling each other. Great, just great.

I awoke with a hangover the size of Vermont. My brain pressed so urgently against my eyes that they were in danger of being ejected like spent shells. I almost blacked out when I touched off my shotgun, and the shriek of a dog whistle was like a spike being driven through my ears. Adrian, who I swear was weaned on hard cider, suffered no ill effects whatsoever. He missed every bird he fired at that morning, while I killed a limit of woodcock.

I do not prescribe a hangover as a shooting slump remedy, although I was tempted to try it two years later. I arrived a half-day before Adrian, in time to check out a choice bit of woodcock cover wedged between a road and a bend in the river. Zack struck point immediately, and I tumbled a left-crossing 'cock.

"This is going to be good," I thought smugly. It might have been for someone else, but it wasn't for me. Zack pointed woodcock after woodcock, and I missed the hell out of all of them. I should have had a limit in fifteen minutes. Instead, I limited out on frustration, despair, and anguish, none of which can be glazed with wild grape jelly and served over wild rice. I pledged my eternal gratitude to Zack for not lifting his leg on me. The Peshtigo is always beautiful, but not always kind.

This was also the year for the infamous "hash grays." Adrian's wife, Janelle, had decided to come along, and one evening she cheerfully announced that hash browns were on the dinner menu. While I heated oil in the skillet, she shredded the potatoes. Outwardly, they appeared to be normal, everyday spuds. In fact, they were the Potatoes From Another Planet. A blow torch wouldn't have turned them brown. We cooked them, and cooked them, and cooked them some more. Nothing happened. Finally, they went all gray and rubbery. None of us had the stomach to taste them. We offered the hash grays to the dogs, who looked at us with expressions that said, "You've got to be kidding." In retrospect, we probably could have made a fortune if we'd sold them to Goodyear.

In 1987, our trip to Peshtigo coincided with four inches of snow and a high pressure system direct from the Arctic Circle. Other than an evening spent clinging to the side of New Hampshire's Mount Washington, I've never been so cold for so long as I was the two nights we shivered away in camp. Adrian's contact lenses froze solid. The water in the dogs' bucket froze solid. The campground pump froze solid. Ade rigged a tarp to trap extra heat from the fire, and we edged as close as we dared to the flames, bundled up and hunched over like ice fishermen. Intermittently, one of us would cry "Safari!" through chattering teeth, in reference to the name of the low-rent – but warm – motel in Wabeno. We persevered. It helped to have Zack sleeping between us in the tent: it was like having a fur rug to snuggle into.

Given the conditions, the hunting was remarkably good. The woodcock were still present in decent numbers, and we couldn't walk to the campground privy without flushing grouse – literally. In a new covert just over the hill from the camp, Ade made one of the most spectacular shots on grouse I'll ever see. Zack pointed on a gentle slope clustered with young aspens. While Ade stayed below on the path, I slithered in to flush. The grouse must have run. It lifted far ahead, and I turned to watch it sail over the spindly trees, safely out of range. Then Ade's little SKB barked spitefully. The grouse cartwheeled into the snow, stone dead. I was stunned.

"You got it! You got it!" I hollered, crashing through the underbrush. Ade just stood there regarding his shotgun with the same kind of wide-eyed amazement the Indians must have displayed when they first witnessed the magical power of the white man's thundersticks. The Red gods had smiled upon him. In the Peshtigo Country, they often do.

As much as it belongs to us, the Peshtigo belongs to the setters. And as intimately as we think we know it, they know it even better.

Maggie – loving, incorrigible, doomed Maggie – made that first trip, never to return. Gabe, now retired, would take your breath away when she pointed, leaning into the scent as if it were a gale, tail kissing the sky. She made her share of game, and although we spent as much time hunting for her as we did for birds – gunning behind Gabe was always an adventure in geography – we have nothing but fond memories of her performances.

Emmy's debut could not have been less auspicious: her inaugural morning in camp, she wandered off, became disoriented, and got lost. We burned up the forest roads frantically searching. Another hunter found her eight miles to the southwest, scared but unhurt, and after phoning my wife (thank God she accepted a collect call from a stranger), he contacted the Forest Service in Laona. The Samaritan delivered Emmy safe and sound, and refused my offer of a "finder's fee." It was here, a year later, that Emmy came into her own as a woodcock dog, striking point after point, literally within sight of the river.

And then there is Zack. He's made every trip: Adrian still laughs over waking in the tent to the sight of Zack peering down on him like a jowly vulture. I cannot imagine hunting the Peshtigo country without this hard-headed old setter. His bell plays the musical score that accompanies our days in the woods. How many times have Ade and I strained to hear that copper bell as it faded in and out, only to be galvanized into action by the *beep-beep-beep* of his Tracker?

How many times have we fought though the hazel and the blackberries and the balsams, losing our hats, to find him on point, head high, nose drinking scent, the bird mesmerized? We've played out hundreds of these small, tense dramas, each as luminous and finely crafted as a scene by Truffaut. In a very real sense, Zack is the agent responsible for revealing the secrets of the Peshtigo to us. Through him, we see beyond the surface, and into its reclusive, enthralling soul.

I was told just the other day that one of the Ojibway meanings of

Peshtigo is "wild goose." Thinking back to that first trip, when a flock of Canadas rose honking into the moonlight as we made camp, I understand now that the meaning has been plain all along.

– Jim Goetz

Larry Van Goethem is a former journalist, having served as city editor of The Janesville Gazette *and as environmental reporter and assistant city editor with* The Milwaukee Journal.

While in these positions, he contributed a series of op-ed essays to The New York Times *and marks those pieces as the start of his writing career. Some of the essays were included in a book,* The Fifth Horseman is Riding, *which was submitted by its publisher, Macmillan, for a Pulitzer Prize in 1974.*

Since then, his articles have appeared in Reader's Digest, National Wildlife *and* Sports Afield, *as well as regional publications and many major daily newspapers.*

Van Goethem and his wife, Bette, who have three daughters, operate a pet boarding kennel near Eagle River, where they raise Shetland sheepdogs. Van Goethem, a fitness walker on roads around his home, also likes classical music and scenic photography.

Ed Poss and the Windigo
by
Larry Van Goethem

In high summer Ed Poss and Dan Nicholson would fish the spring holes after supper and if the trout brooded, as they often do, Nicholson would say, "When the mosquitoes start to agree, it's Royal Coachman time."

"Well, you know," Poss said, "I realized after a while that he wasn't reminding us of the rule, he was reciting a litany so the trout would bite."

Sometime after that, years after Nicholson died, Poss encountered him again. This was well past Royal Coachman time, but I'll get to that – and the Windigo – in a minute or so. First a bit about Poss.

To understand Poss you must realize that he was one of a vanishing breed, a woods rat. Such men are looked down upon these days but once they were objects of rural veneration, respected for their lore if not learning. Henry David Thoreau was a Harvard man who took post-graduate work in the Concord woods.

Thoreau liked fishermen, hunters, loggers and such – and why not? In them is a rude poetry of the still, dancing snow, the loon's tremolo, the brittle cry of the fox, the whistle of deer in the swamps and a ruffed grouse's burst of flight.

Living close to the earth as they do, woods rats acquire a mystical sense of primitive origins, of earthen gods and foul spirits . . . of ghosts.

But, like Thoreau, Poss was really a townsman living a country life. He had a job with the Antigo Fire Department and, as rural people say, he "minded the store." That is, he paid the bills, raised three daughters, and saved money.

Money was sufficient to keep Ed and his wife, Priscilla, comfortable after cancer and arthritis crippled Ed beyond repair. Bedridden until his death, Poss saw his days withering into a long night, turned over his time in the woods like a video, thought about departed cronies . . . and roamed the hills again.

"I've fished and hunted pretty much every place in this country," he said of his northern Wisconsin home. "That was the curse," he reflected. "That was really a curse. Instead of having wider horizons, I'd head out to the woods. But you can't cure that. It's an obsession. You don't feel right unless you're out in the woods."

He was alive there. "Something about getting out in the woods alone," he said. "In winter it's about the best experience there is. It's still; you see more things. All of your senses are alert."

Maybe too alert. He sometimes felt another presence, knew when he was being observed, felt the flesh rising on his arms, could smell deer. He believes in spirits. Having been alone so often in remote places, Poss arrived at the autumn of his years aware – indeed, insistent – that he was never really alone.

"There are things we don't know much about," he suggested.

Ed was prone to make such statements in his later years, but, then, those are the mysteries we begin to plumb as we age. Everything seems so obvious to the young. Me, I was 50 before I encountered my first ghost – at least, I should qualify, one that I recognized.

The old man shared his wisdom – not forgetting his follies, which he freely admitted – via a network of telephone cronies with whom he visited every day. I made his list because I was a writer, hence generally available. It didn't bother him when I hinted that I had a hot manuscript going; he'd visit with me anyway and I came to realize that the time spent in those meandering conversations was old gold.

Sometimes an old man mellows like fine wine and sharpens like the best cheddar. All of the ego and pride is stripped away as presumptive intelligence is replaced by wisdom as sweet as the sap running in March sugar maples. Ed's most vivid recollections were selfless, such as his encounters with spirits, one the ghost of an old friend and the other being a Windigo.

Poss encountered the ghost on a twilight summer evening when he was coming out of Rasmussen Springs, once a favored trout hole.

"You know how the Kentucky fog rolls in," he said. "Well, I was walking back to the road. There's this old logging road under the trees. It's almost like a tunnel there and it was dim. There was an old lumber camp in that meadow. I saw a disturbance in the air, something in the fog. Then something knocked my cap off. I didn't know what it was, but it wasn't a tree. I was really shaken then. I ran the rest of the way to the car. I didn't go back. My boat is still there."

What was it?

"It was Dan Nicholson. He and I spent a lot of time together. He died of cancer. His wife did too."

How does he know it was Nicholson?

"I know who it was." He said this without further embellishment – take it or leave it. Dan was a freebooter, he said. "Dan and I . . . he would do something like that."

Besides his boat, the fishing cap is still there, Poss never having cared to retrieve it, never returning to the haunted old lumber camp.

Of all the places that Poss frequented, his favorite was the Hunting River, which rises near Elcho and runs into the Wolf River after a beguiling journey through woodland, marshes and old meadows.

"The Hunting meadows are calling me," Poss cried out one lovely September afternoon when the memory of trout and their lairs was upon him. "The Hunting is missing me. The meadows of the Hunting are calling me."

He once found an early snowfall there, the snow like whipped cream on higher ground, falling suddenly to the river's marsh grass, still so vividly green that the contrast was unearthly.

"That was the closest to reverence I have ever come," he said.

The Hunting was where Poss and the Windigo matched wills.

Windigos were monster ice men, feared and loathed by woodland Indians. The Cree said.they were 20 to 30 feet tall, with bodies of ice, and devoured humans.

Chippewas regarded Windigos as giant hominid spirits lurking at the edges of their lives, indeed their very campfires, usually just beyond comprehension, let alone reality . . . but always at the remote ends of bitter journeys.

If a Chippewa brave did not return from a hunt, he was presumed to have been eaten by a Windigo. A hunter following a strange track, not that of man or beast, journeyed into oblivion. Poss believes he escaped a fatal confrontation.

The day Poss saw the Windigo, he was sitting by the Hunting, musing on the day and its portents.

"I was watching some wood ducks scooting along. You know how you get engrossed. Then I thought I'd put them to flight and I stood up and yelled, but instead of flying they came scooting over to me. I sez, even the ducks aren't afraid of me. I didn't know it then but they had seen the Windigo.

"I was taking my gear apart when I looked over to this clearing and there was a cloud. I looked a little closer and this Windigo was looking at me. It appeared in rising fog. Well – I took off running and I could feel its breath on my neck. It was rough going on the swamp hummocks. Finally I got to high ground and I turned around and let out a mighty roar.

"And I could tell that all nature was in accord with me because the wind started blowing in the popples, and the leaves were saying, 'Oh no, Windigo! Oh no! Go, Windigo, go!' And the birds were singing, 'Oh, oh Windigo. No.' And I heard Old 82, the time freight, and its whistle was wailing, 'Oh no, Windigo. Go.' When I looked back I could see the evil one sneaking away on the evening mist and I knew that I would have no more trouble with it for a long time to come."

Having survived such a quaking hazard, Poss felt it necessary to fortify himself with other kinds of spirits, so he stopped at a country tavern on the way home, arriving home tipsy to a cool wife.

"They never understand," he explained.

The genesis of a woods rat is peculiar. Poss had a stern father who believed a boy was grown up at 16 and should get all A's. Poss played hookey from school to fish and got C's. During the thirties he rode the rails around the country, looking for work, part of the army of bums created by the Depression.

When he was on the bum, Poss returned home but there was never any work so he'd "shack out" in the woods, hunting and fishing and berrying to stay alive.

He married Priscilla after his hound got into the habit of wandering off. Priscilla would collar the dog and return it to Poss, which is how one thing led to another.

When the workaday life began he retreated to the woods after work. Sometimes he'd snowshoe into the Prairie River deer yards to see how the deer were wintering. He never found anybody's tracks but his own there. He was a man born out of his time and place. Put him in a westering America and he would have lit out for the mountains. Trout fly fishing was an addiction.

He was casual about spirits. When I told him about strange tracks I was seeing in the woods he was concerned. The tracks had hooves like a deer, but they also had single, claw-like protrusions.

"My friend, you are a marked man," Poss said.

"What in the world do you mean?" I asked.

"The Windigo," he said. "Be sure to wear old clothing when you're out there."

"Why?"

"It breathes fire. It'll ruin your good clothes." A pause, then: "Asbestos helps."

When I asked him what the Windigo looked like, he searched for words.

"It was like miasma," he finally said. "You think I'm lying?" he challenged. "Haven't I told the truth about everything else?"

Many older hunters will understand why Poss stopped hunting. He killed his last deer in 1962, and he put it to me this way: "As a guy gets older, he mellows. You hate to kill deer. I don't want to kill anything. The closer to death you come, the less you want to kill something."

This is why he watched the spikehorn buck drift past his stand during his last hunting season, never lifted his carbine – yes, an old Winchester – stood up and said to hell with it and hiked out to the road.

"I never went back," he mused.

In his final years when Priscilla had to get him in and out of bed and wheelchair, feed him and attend to his toilet, Poss had a grand vision to witness; it was nothing less than his life.

"I've been to all of the places that I've seen," he says. "In your mind's eye you go back over some of those places, which you know like the back of your hand, experiences you've had."

Poss had a valve replaced in his heart in 1976, a pig valve. "Those are only good for about ten years," he observed with laconic calm. "So I guess I'm on borrowed time."

Not long before his death he told a daughter in a letter, "It isn't Royal Coachman time forever."

I will miss Poss when his trout stop rising, but expect to see him around after he's gone . . . somewhere. Meantime, I take a stick when I walk these days. Never know what you might see out there.

– Sandy Klein Stevens

Richard Behm is a trout fisherman, grouse hunter, and poet, husband of Mary, father of teenage daughter Jessica, and professor of English at the University of Wisconsin-Stevens Point (not necessarily in order of importance). He has won three creative writing fellowships from the Wisconsin Arts Board, most recently for fiction writing in 1993. His outdoor writing has appeared in Sporting Classics, Gray's Sporting Journal, Sports Afield, Field & Stream, Wisconsin Sportsman, Petersen's Hunting Annual, and elsewhere. He believes the Chequamegon National Forest is "full of haunted and sacred places."

First Fish: Of Fathers and Their Children

by
Richard Behm

I have before me a picture of my daughter, Jessica, when she was no more than four. She is holding a stringer of very small sunfish. The photograph conveys her conflicting feelings. She is smiling, green eyes under blonde hair, and proud, yet her entire body is curved away from the tangle of finny creatures waving their life away in the July sunlight. I recall I filleted the fish and we ate them with french fries – lots of french fries.

She remembers nothing of it, and by the time she was old enough to really enjoy fishing with me, she entered her anti-killing stage. We'd go round and round about the fact that sometimes I killed animals and ate them. She'd suffer through my "A Big Mac is just a dead cow" lecture, and I'd listen to her "Fish have feelings, too" sermon.

We reached the nadir in our discussions when she was twelve and we took a trip to the Boundary Waters Canoe Area with some friends. She insisted that I release a four-pound smallmouth because it was fighting to get back to its children. I explained, in a not-too-patient voice, that the fish was more likely to eat her young, if she could, than sing them a song and tuck them into bed.

Tears streamed down Jessica's face. I released the fish. Some things are more important than being right and winning an argument.

At fourteen, she became a vegetarian. It took the two of us awhile, but eventually we reached an uneasy truce. She would refrain from criticizing my sporting activities and I would try my best to not point out inconsistencies in her position, such as the thigh-high leather boots she bought one year. (The animal was dead anyway; my lecture on supply and demand fell on deaf ears.) Our relationship seems to have survived, and she has come to understand something of why I hunt and fish, finding a sense in my explanations that she does not find in commercial activities such as factory farming. She's pretty sure she knows everything, and maybe she does. I knew a lot more when I was sixteen than I do at forty.

I knew, for instance, that I didn't want to be my father, that whatever his strengths, I wanted to be somebody different, to make my own way and my own mark in the world. And yet, the reason I hunt and fish is rooted somewhere deep in my own childhood, in the beauty of the early relationship between father and son, and the uncertain relationship that has grown up since then.

The first fish I remember catching was a bullhead pulled from the cold night waters of a Wisconsin lake where my family was vacationing. I was eight or so. An image of my father survives from that night; he was sitting on the sandy beach, watching me and my younger brother, Steve, making sure we didn't step off the end of the dock. "Be careful!" he'd admonish as we'd lean out into the watery darkness. I can still see the ruby glow of his cigar in the dark, make out his silhouette against the shore.

We were fishing bobbers as big as our little-boy fists, with worms below and a ton of sinkers tied on, enough to provide ballast for a lake steamer, enough so that we could cast our gob of worm at least ten feet before the line snarled on our open-face reels and the entire mess landed like a meteor.

We were excited, watching our bobbers dance in the moonlight that spilled like a pirate's booty – silver and gold, sapphire and emerald – over the water. We'd shine our Commander flashlights to follow our bobbers being pulled out into the lake, or beneath the dock or toward the cattails along the shore, and pull up twisting, angry bullheads. Dad would to come out on the dock to help us take them from the hook and put another worm on.

So this was fishing! A huge Wisconsin sky, moonlight, and fierce, magic creatures pulled from the water by our own hands. For the first time I knew how the pulse quickened, how breath comes in gasps, learned something of the communion between fish and man, life and death. In the background sat my father, watching us dance on the end of that rickety dock.

My father put the fish on a stringer tied to the back of the rowboat that came with the cottage we'd rented. In the morning he skinned them and rolled them in flour and cornmeal. For breakfast, we ate bacon and eggs and the fish my brother and I had caught. We had never eaten a more delicious breakfast.

I am sure dad took us fishing other times, though my recollections are murky at best. I do know that because of him, fishing became a part of my secret childhood, creating the fantasy places I escaped to along the Sandusky River; a dark limestone cavern, a railroad trestle, a waterfall. I never caught any of the game fish inhabiting the river that slices through northern Ohio to Lake Erie – walleye, smallmouth, white bass. I never even managed to hook a carp, though I often paused to marvel at their huge, silver carcasses discarded along the shore. With a pussywillow I poked their bellies, thick with flies and maggots. The flies would buzz, then settle back into the cavity. Carp were beautiful and death was amazing.

I also remember fishing a feeder creek to the Sandusky, a creek that winds through what was then the Tiffin State Hospital for the Mentally Insane – or some other such impressive name. My dad and all the other adults simply called it The Nuthouse. ("You know, Sophie was out to The Nuthouse for a while.")

For us children, however, The Nuthouse held a special attraction. There was a beautiful little falls within the hospital grounds, and below it a pool where we would fish for sunfish as lovely as those my daughter holds in the photograph.

In my mind I can still see the mist rising from the falls, smell the dampness of the stone, and feel the small, mad tug of a fish on the rusty hook baited with a worm dug from the backyard the night before. One day I brought home an ice cream pail of small panfish, most having no more meat than a walleye cheek. Still, my dad praised the catch and cleaned and cooked the fish for us.

Steve and I also fished at the bull farm pond, a muddy circle located on the grounds of the Northern Ohio Breeders Association. Like The Nuthouse, the bull farm pond was a place we liked as much for the excitement of fishing forbidden waters as for the chance of catching fish of note.

All the Breeder's Association pond held, appropriately, were bull-heads. But we knew we were not allowed to fish there, and so the fishing was especially daring. To make it more exciting, we fantasized that we were always in danger from the bulls, when in truth they were behind a gnarl of barbed wire on the other side of a building. Then, as now, the illusion sustained us – imminent danger and the possibility of a big fish. How often, wading a wilderness trout stream at dusk, I have almost captured that same rush of fear and possibility.

My father warned us against fishing at the pond, though he seemed more concerned that we might be caught than be hurt by an enraged bull. Yet the warning never elevated into a major scolding or punishment of the kind my brother and I received for painting the seat of Angie Ballreich's new bicycle silver. Perhaps, in his grown-up heart, heavy with the demands of building a small business, dad envied our escapades.

I stopped fishing somewhere along the line, simply gave it up the way I did baseball and trains, model airplanes and my rock collection. But with that putting away of childish things, I also put away longings and emotions, dreams and beliefs; and in that difference, the relationship between father and son changed.

After early childhood, the rituals of American fathers and sons often become complicated and are rarely graceful. I know a few men who have sustained visible affection for their fathers, and the fathers for the sons, beyond childhood; who share a kind of camaraderie. It's something I both envy and scorn: envy a closeness I have lost, scorn a relationship I've been taught can exist only at a subterranean level – unarticulated, disguised, expressed (if at all) only in superficial ways.

The nature of modern American adolescence is such that for many, myself included, each small act of rebellion is another petty brick laid in place in the wall that separates father from son, man from man. And once the wall is up, it is just too damn big to get over very often without great emotional effort. I've tried to get over that wall a few times, but neither hard enough nor long enough. If I ever succeeded in breaching the wall, I'm not sure I'd know what to do. The wall's been there so long that both my father and I take it for granted. It is part of what defines our relationship, a kind of lurking, monolithic totem around which we both dance.

My eyes return to my daughter's picture, the delicate curve of her pink-clad body away from the squirming mass of golden fish, her cryptic, twisted smile. I wonder what the world holds for her, for us; how we will relate to each other as she enters adulthood. Jessica, sixteen now, is assuming her woman shape and identity. Much of her life is a mystery to me. As far as I can tell, the major role I serve for her right now is to be taken for granted. I'm to be in the background, but there, rock-solid, if she needs me. I think my father would know what I am talking about. Though distances opened between us and I did my share of wall-building, I knew he was there should I fall.

I came back to fishing when I was attending graduate school in Ohio, a few miles away from where I grew up. As they say, a lot of water had passed under the bridge. I had a wife, Jessica was less than a year old, my mother had died of lung cancer two years earlier, and I was trying to take my graduate exams for English literature, finish a dissertation, and get a job before my GI Bill benefits ran out.

Driving around one day, I found a muddy creek with a path beside it, and I followed the path to a glade of shadows and emerald ferns, luminous with an almost ethereal light. In the creek, a huge fish leaped out of the water. Someone was running a trot line baited with what I took to be chicken guts. I pulled it up, and two large catfish writhed on hooks.

So to this glade I would go with a cheap, discount store rod and reel and a can of worms I had dug myself. I would sit there, fishing, reading aloud, memorizing dozens of poems: W. B. Yeats' "The Lake Isle of Innisfree," John Dunne's "Death, Be Not Proud," William Blake's "The Tyger," Shakespeare's sonnet "That Time of Year Thou Mays't in Me Behold," whose final couplet echoes down the years:

This thou perceiv'st, which makes thy love more strong,
To love that well which thou must leave ere long.

Sometimes one of those monster catfish would leap from the water, shaking itself in the gloomy light. I never had a single bite, but I passed my graduate exams.

Then I took a teaching job in Wisconsin, where I had begun fishing with my father, years before. Fishing seemed a way of life here. It wasn't long until a friend talked me into forsaking my worms for a fly rod, and my life changed dramatically. I found in fly-fishing a joy that transcends the routine of life; that in its esoteric art of feathers and bamboo, its arcane knowledge of insects and the ways of the trout, its rhythms of water and – when practiced well – its balances and harmonies, re-establishes a link with the grand circle of earth, water, air, life, and death.

These are not things, however, I can share with my father, who, though he took my brother and me fishing, never fished much himself. I thought that after he retired he would take up fishing as a hobby, but he has shown no interest. I see him only once or twice a year, write him occasionally, phone on holidays. Ours is a classic American post-nuclear family – blown all over the continent.

I called this last Father's Day. He sounded well, but said he wasn't. My brother got on the line and said, "Well, you know how the Old Man is." The Old Man. I suppose – I hope – I'll live to hear my daughter refer to me with such respectful irreverence.

What I'd really like to do is take my dad fishing, give back to him the precious gift he gave to me. I want him to feel the throb of a sixteen-inch brown trout taken on a fly I've tied – no, that he's tied – in a misty stream while the moon climbs overhead. I want him to feel the joy and excitement, every bit as vivid as that long-ago bullhead. Perhaps unknowingly, he gave a special gift to me one night on a star-strewn Wisconsin lake. Father. Hookbaiter. Fish cleaner. Protector. If only we could go back to that magic, moon-struck night of first fish, when the world seemed whole and each fish was a promise someone would keep.

~

– Sharon Anderson

George Vukelich contributes two columns weekly to Isthmus *of Madison and a monthly column to* Wisconsin Outdoor Journal. *He also hosts the program "Pages from a North Country Notebook" Sunday nights on Wisconsin Public Radio.*

His environmental essays have appeared in numerous newspapers and magazines and have been honored by Milwaukee Press Club awards, the Gordon MacQuarrie Award from the Wisconsin Academy of Sciences, Arts, and Letters, and the Outdoor Writing Award from the Council of Wisconsin Writers.

Vukelich is also the author of Fisherman's Beach, *a novel about the life and struggles of a commercial fishing family on Lake Michigan.*

Coming of Age
by
George Vukelich

Connie sat there on the old jack-pine stump that had been his personal deer stand for the last 25 years and talked to himself the way old hunters who are also old grandpas do.

"This will be the worst damn deer hunt you have ever been on, Conrad. You will be in pure hell before this day is over and you've got nobody to blame but yourself because you brought it on."

He shifted the rifle in his lap and peered at the fringe of the cedar swamp in which, at this very moment, Bill and the grandsons were slithering and stumbling in their misbegotten attempts to get old grandpa a shot at a deer.

The cedar swamp was as serene as church. To Connie, it always looked like those autumnal scenes of the leafless Wisconsin woods that Mel Kishner used to paint for the Sunday *Milwaukee Journal* at the beginning of deer season.

The quiet in the swamp meant that Bill and the boys probably hadn't started their drive yet. Most likely because they wanted to make sure that grandpa was in place on his stump – all settled in, his breathing back to normal after the long trek from the cabin, his gun loaded and ready.

They probably were figuring in enough time for grandpa to have a coffee out of the thermos to get him sensitized and alert for the trophy buck they promised to flush out for him.

"You got to be really wired today, grandpa," Chuckie had warned him as he had poured the breakfast coffee. "You're gonna see more deer than you saw in the last five years. We're talking Action City!"

Connie didn't feel a need to pour anything out of the thermos. He didn't need to get himself 'wired.' God, just to be out here, sitting on a stump and just breathing that crisp air of the country was excitement enough. Of course, how the hell could you explain that to somebody half your age, as Bill was, or somebody from a different planet altogether, as Bill's boys were?

It was something he couldn't talk about because nobody in the deer camp was his age.

"Say it," he said to himself. "Nobody here is as old as you are and how can you expect anybody younger to understand what the hell's happening to you?"

What was happening to him, he really didn't understand himself. It had started happening three, four deer seasons back and he hadn't told anybody about it until he had told Doc just this last summer.

Doc had never been much of a hunter, not deer or birds or anything. He fished trout and that was pretty much it. But Doc was never judgmental about hunters and you could talk to Doc about the serious stuff like growing old and life and death because that's what Doc dealt with all the time. Plus – and it was a big plus – Doc and Connie were the same age and had gone through a lot of the same stuff together, like school and the Army and arthritis.

"It's hard to share bladder problems with the teenie-boppers," Doc said.

Connie just knew that he was going to share his problem with Doc because he had to share it with someone, and who the hell else was there? Some way, somehow, he would find a way to just bring it into the conversation and share it. He really felt like he was going through a change of life or something.

It was at Connie's birthday party last summer that the opportunity arose. They were in the backyard having brats and beer and a birthday cake with one candle. It was a tradition since Connie had turned 60, some seasons back.

"Makes sense," Doc said. "After all, you're only celebrating this birthday today. You've already celebrated the rest. Who the hell needs a forest fire?"

It was the present from Bill and the grandsons that did Connie in. Everybody raved about the thoughtfulness and the originality. It was a birthday card with a magnificent deer in watercolors.

"Grandpa," the card read. "This card entitles you to the best deer hunt of your life this season. We will drive the cedar swamp until you get THE FIRST DEER THIS YEAR. PERIOD. Happy Birthday from 'the Swamp Rats'."

It was signed by his four grandsons and Bill.

That's when Conrad cornered Doc for a talk.

"Well," Doc said, "it's easy to see where they got their genes. You must be touched and I am impressed. They're saying that grandpa gets his deer before anybody gets a deer. They love their grandpa. Not too shabby, Conrad."

"They're doing it," Connie said, "because grandpa didn't get a deer the last couple of seasons."

"So, this year," Doc said, "they're making sure grandpa gets his deer. Grandpa doesn't like that?"

"Doc," Connie said. "I've been going out there and just sitting on my stump and I really don't care if I never shoot another deer in my life."

Connie sat as silent as a partridge for a spell.

"The reason I didn't get a deer the last four seasons," he said finally, "is that I've been sitting there with an empty gun."

The look on Doc's face hadn't been there since the time he hooked an owl on his back cast.

"An empty gun?"

"That's right," Connie said. "An empty gun. Unloaded. I knew I wasn't going to shoot it so why the hell should I load it?"

"You know," Doc said, "that's like fishing without a hook. That's really pretty funny, Conrad."

"Actually," Connie said, "the first two seasons I loaded the gun I even shot it in the air to fool them. Then, of course, I had to clean the damn gun and I thought, 'Boy, how dumb can you get?'"

"Conrad, Conrad," Doc said gently. "And you bought the licenses and the deer tags and everything."

"I'll tell you, Doc," Connie said, "don't think I haven't felt like a damn fool out there. Deer are going by you like cows going to the barn and you have to pretend – you have to lie – about not seeing any deer or not having a good clear shot available.

"Why couldn't I just come right out and tell them that it was just getting hard for me to kill anymore and all I wanted to do was just sit on my stump and watch the world go by? But if I sat out there without a gun in deer season, you know they'd think Grandpa had gone soft or senile or something.

"Grandpa raised them all to hunt and what happens if hunting isn't important to grandpa anymore?"

"You can't tell Bill?"

"What the hell could I say? Especially after all this time. I just put it off and put it off and got by and all of a sudden you just can't put it off anymore."

"Like a trip to the doctor," Doc said.

"It's just gotten harder for me to kill," Connie said. "That's what it really is – and I was ashamed to tell anybody about it. Isn't that terrible? My own family."

Doc didn't really answer until about a week later. He mailed Connie a photocopy of some pages from *Wisconsin Trails* magazine.

There was a handwritten note in Doc's prescription scrawl:

"We were straightening up our magazine selection in the waiting room and thought this applied to your case. Mel Ellis, as you probably know, was an outdoor writer for *The Milwaukee Journal* before he turned legit and wrote books. This is from an interview circa 1971. Take two aspirin and call me in the morning."

Connie smiled and read. It was like hearing a friend talk to him over a coffee.

"It's getting tough for me to kill," Mel Ellis had said back in 1971. "I've got a theory that eventually no one will shoot anything or kill anything. It's just a matter of becoming civilized.

"We've been hunters so long we don't know what else to be. Someday we are going to be civilized, but it's going to be another thousand, two thousand, five thousand years. If man is still around then, he is going to be civilized."

Connie knew now that Mel Ellis' words had gotten to him. Connie liked to think that they got to him in the same way a grain of sand gets to an oyster and the oyster then forms a pearl around that grain.

He felt the sun toasting his cheeks. He inhaled the still, chill air, cold as trout water. He poured a half cup from the steaming thermos and waited.

The first deer materialized in the swamp fringe. The rack on its head was as big as an elk's. It stood still, ears flicking, listening. It trotted toward him casually, never seeing him.

"Hello," Connie said, and the deer just exploded straight up in the air, it looked like ten feet, and bounded past him like a kangaroo. Connie thought he saw fear in the deer's eyes. Then again, it might have been only disbelief.

He could hear yells and shouting coming from the swamp and suddenly deer began appearing like apparitions. One here. One there. Two. Three at a time. God, Connie thought. It was like watching a colony of field mice being flushed by the barn cats.

What a drive his boys were putting on in that jungle. He knew what it took out of you to drive like that and he was washed in guilt because they were doing it for him. Getting grandpa a deer that grandpa didn't want to shoot.

But he was so damn proud of them because they were doing something for somebody else, sweating and falling down and getting wet and scratched and he hoped that they at least saw some of the magnificent animals moving like shadows away from them.

Connie sat there, sipping his coffee and marveling at the show the boys had provided. I should have filmed it, he thought. Yeah, that's all you need, he told himself. So they could see the deer coming out of the swamp like rabbits and nobody shooting.

Maybe somebody would shoot grandpa and they could film that.

The deer all disappeared to the north. By late afternoon, those that hadn't been shot would have doubled back to bed down in the cedar for another night.

It was almost ten minutes before the next apparition came out of the swamp. It was Bill. He stood still, breathing deeply, his eyes seeking his father, surveying the area around the stump, looking for a downed deer, a blood trail, something. Then, he walked slowly up the rise to Connie, his eyes watching the ground all the way, seeing the deep tracks in the soft soil.

"I didn't hear any shots from you," Bill said. "They must have come through here like rabbits."

He hunkered down at Connie's knees and shook his head.

"They busted their buns in this drive and you just sat here and never fired your gun? Are you all right, Pa? I mean, you didn't have a seizure or a blackout or something?"

"I'm all right," Connie said. "Here."

He handed Bill his rifle.

"Did you unload it?" Bill asked.

"No," Connie said.

Bill worked back the bolt-action on the ancient .30-30 and his eyes got big as an owl's.

"It's empty," he said.

"I never loaded it," Connie said.

Figures in blaze orange were emerging from the cedar swamp. They stood as their father had stood only moments before, breathing deeply, their eyes seeking their Grandpa, surveying the area around his stump, looking for a downed deer, a blood trail, something.

They walked slowly up the rise to Connie's stump, their eyes watching the ground all the way, seeing the deep tracks in the soft soil.

"God, Grandpa," Chuckie said, "it looks like a buffalo herd came through here. What happened? You hit any?"

"Well," Bill said quickly, "you're not gonna believe this, but this was so much fun, Grandpa wants to do this again next year."

Connie looked at the faces of his grandsons, sweaty, bewildered. Chuck had angry scratches that had drawn blood.

Connie just wanted to cry and hold them all, but that would only embarrass them. Instead, he passed around the paper cups and poured them coffee.

"Well," he said finally, "your dad was kidding about the next year part, I think. You know where he gets that mother wit. From his mother, of course. But, he was right about one thing . . ."

Connie took a deep slow breath, the same deep, slow breath he had always taken to relax himself, to steady himself as he squeezed off the trigger on the .30-30.

"Your dad's right about that one thing," Connie said to his grandsons. "You are not going to believe this."

ॐ

– Paul Birling

Susan K. Wendorf took up the outdoor life at an early age. She remembers her grandfather eating breakfast the night before they went fishing so they could get an earlier start in the morning. The family album has a black-and-white print of Susan, not quite three, fishing at Shawano Lake, cane pole in hand and a can of worms beside her. Today her favorite spot is the Chippewa Flowage, which she has fished for more than 15 years.

A former Lutheran clergywoman who served parishes in Platteville, Cross Plains, and Thiensville, Wendorf has been a family law paralegal and is now a Family Mediation Counselor in Jefferson County. She has written more than a dozen devotional booklets, newspaper articles, essays, and Biblical studies. "Up North" is her first published outdoor work.

She is a graduate of Valparaiso University, Yale University Divinity School, and Lutheran School of Theology, Chicago. A Milwaukee native, Susan now lives in Oconomowoc with a friend and her schnoodle, Molly Putzer.

Up North
by
Susan K. Wendorf

Like a winter chickadee flitting from branch to feeder to fir, Up North refuses to settle down in one place. Up North may be Minocqua or Metonga, Crivitz or Couderay, Shawano or Shell Lake. Up North defies delineation but welcomes discovery, as long as you know what you're looking for.

If you live in New Berlin, Newburg definitely is not Up North – but New London has real possibilities. From Platteville to Plain isn't quite far enough to be truly Up North, but Pittsville is a shoo-in. There is a line – a latitude attitude – that must be found and crossed before you can claim Up North, but you won't find it marked on any map. Perhaps that's what makes Up North so difficult to define: it's more a place in the soul, a state of mind, than a place.

It's a complete enigma to those unfamiliar with the ways of

Wisconsin. People who live in California can say they're going to the ocean and know when they've arrived. They can put a bare toe into it, watch the water surge and roll, listen to the waves' dialects and announce with certainty, "This is the ocean!" People who live in Pennsylvania can say they're going to the mountains, choose a highway, and know they're at the mountains' feet when all they can do is look up. They say to their relatives from Indiana, "These are the mountains," and no one disputes them. But if you live in Wisconsin and you're thinking Up North, there are a hundred ways to get there. A thousand people can make the journey and not one of them need claim the same place, all for different reasons.

Thinking Up North is almost as important as going Up North; it is definitely a requisite first step. If you don't have the time to allow your mind to wander to the back bay where you saw the bear bathing, perhaps you need to reassess your real reasons for going Up North in the first place. If you're disinclined to re-catch that five-pound walleye a thousand times between visits; if you're too busy to let your memory set you down on a pier at sunrise; if things more important prevent you from floating your well-rehearsed footsteps along the path to that wild berry patch, perhaps your going Up North is too hastily preempting your thinking Up North. It's a strange marriage: you can't think Up North until you've been there, but from then on it isn't quite right to go Up North until you've sufficiently thought about it.

But if you think you see, on Monday evening, the moon shimmering on the water at the Chippewa Flowage when in fact it's just a reflection of the street light on the bird bath in you're backyard, be warned: you're thinking Up North. If, on Wednesday, you seem to feel beneath your feet the springy sponge of the forest floor when in truth it's the new carpeting in the den, take heed: you're thinking Up North. If you think you hear, early Thursday morning, the plaintive cry of the loon when in fact it was just . . . well, nothing imitates the loon, but when you're thinking Up North everything calls to you.

I go Up North as often as I can but it never seems to be often enough. My soul resides there; it is the place of the "other me" in much the same way, I suspect, as is the life forming within the womb of a pregnant woman. There is there a sacredness, a wholly otherness that I've found nowhere else. Those who know Up North know we take life from the depths of its waters and breath from the far reaches of its open skies and peace from the quaking serenity of its birches. But the relationship is symbiotic, not fungal.

To be fungal to Up North is to only take, never give, never return, replenish, feed, or nurture. To be fungal is to steal the cry of the loon from the evening air, run the dancing frolic of the fawn out of the woods, snatch the stately march of the beaver off the lakeshore, spirit away the soundless attack of the muskie from the sandbar – and leave nothing in return. Or worse, to leave behind the ominous ugliness of so-called civilized society that poisons and strangles and silences that society which existed before us.

To be symbiotic with Up North begins, proceeds, and finally climaxes quite differently. The cry of the loon is not stolen, but received and relished and turned over and over again in the mind's ear. The frolic of the fawn is danced in a whirling of memory's best gifts. The march of the beaver is repeated step by step until the security of dam and house are achieved. The attack of the muskie is celebrated and studied in silent awe, with or without an angler's prayer of success answered.

But always, always, there is in Up North's symbiosis a nurturing of mutual proportions, so that each giver is no more depleted than is the loon for releasing her cry to the night. Both benefit from what the other gives. Neither resents the exchange.

And so I give to Up North myself, confident that I will have me back and even better than before. I give to Up North my love, my respect, my rapt attention, my laughter and delight in the vagaries of its songs and seasons. I rest myself in its past and hope for its future, praising its transitory glory and revering the holiness of its very name.

There are times I've wished I could summon the same reverence for Down Here that I hold for Up North. Down Here brings out the worst in me, Up North the best. Down Here offers me comforts that I placidly appreciate and greedily take for granted. Down Here lulls me into complacent acceptance of screaming headlines and to work, eat, play, sleep in a rhythm that rocks and rumbles on the brink of insanity.

Up North sets me free. Not free from so much as free to. There is no magic in Up North's humble offerings of sight and smell and sound and touch, yet in its very humility there is couched a glimpse of the divine and a taste of healing. Sometimes Up North almost seems embarrassed at my expectations of personal renewal, but I have never been disappointed.

Perhaps "repair" is a better descriptor than "renewal." Renewal brings to mind shining up an old silver reel that has become tarnished; the change is only cosmetic and will not endure. Repair fixes that what has been broken and replaces what has been lost. I most deeply long for Up North when I feel the most broken in soul and spirit, not simply dull and lacking in luster. A polishing cloth will not do for the ache in my being.

I have it on good authority that my first trip Up North was taken at the tender age of five months – *in utero*. And sometimes I wonder: as the water lapped at the sides of the wooden boat my mother sat in while fishing, did womb-waves meet lake-waves to form an unbroken stream from fetus to future? Is that such an absurd possibility? As she and dad worked side by side cleaning perch and bluegill, could the deftness of her hands begin etching in my still-forming brain the feel of flesh on fishbone? When she walked from pier to cottage hauling gear after a day on the lake, is that when I first traced the steps that now I've covered a thousand times myself? We were no strangers to each other, Up North and I, when first we were introduced in the recallable memory. We were old friends from before the day we met.

Don't ask me, don't expect me, to leave Up North willingly or cavalierly after only two or three weeks in the pleasure of its company. When that last morning comes, Up North and I barely talk to each other. I become all business, hoping to insulate myself against the wrenching pain of imminent departure. Up North says little, and in fact more times than not weeps great drops of cold spring rain as I drive down the sandy lane.

My dog barks a warning at my trailered boat following too closely behind us for her sensibilities, but she settles down quickly with the hum of tires meeting asphalt as we head south. I don't think Molly Putzer understands that we are leaving my beloved Up North; her dreaming feet chase northern chipmunks as happily as southern squirrels. She seems content wherever we are, as long as it's with me. I feel a bit guilty not to be sharing her single-minded devotion.

I never know quite when it's going to happen, but I know it will; it must. As boat and Jeep and dog and I travel steadily south, somewhere, at some imprecise but always recognizable moment, we again cross that line that announces we've left Up North. Sometimes it's when we reach the interstate, but not always. Sometimes it's when we turn east for the first time, but not always then, either. Once it was the first McDonald's sign, once the first highway construction site, and once when I turned on the car radio and listened, really listened, to the news.

"Home Is Where You Hang Your Hang-ups," declared a bold poster from my college days in the sixties. "Stay, stay at home, my heart, and rest . . ." counseled Longfellow, as though he knew what he was talking about. Down Here is home for now, and I accept that as it must be. But my spirit, my inmost being, pulls me back Up North time and time again, even if the loons call a million songs between my visits. Up North is always worth the wait. ❧

– Sandy Klein Stevens

Galen Winter was born in Shawano. After World War II US Navy service, he was a member of a United Nations reconstruction team on Walcheren Island in the Netherlands. He later sold clothing to braceros in Arizona, did field work for the Arizona Fish and Game Commission, and lived in Mexico and Puerto Rico while negotiating and managing contracts between US and Latin American corporations.

The US Chamber of Commerce appointed him a delegate to the 1957 Hemispheric Insurance Conference in Caracas, Venezuela. He was a corporation attorney in Milwaukee and Chicago, and is a member of the Illinois, the Chicago, and the Wisconsin Bar Associations. He now practices law in Shawano.

Winter explains all this by muttering about the advantages of living in a place where a man can associate with dogs, guns and fish without arousing too much suspicion and by veiled allusions to the habits of salmon.

Winter writes a column for Shooting Sportsman *magazine that concerns itself with the activities of that consummate shotgunner, Major Nathaniel Peabody, U.S.A.(ret.). His outdoor humor column, "Backlash" is a regular feature in* Wisconsin Outdoor Journal.

Unendangered Species
by
Galen Winter

Sometimes it seems our stewardship of life on this planet has been terribly inept and incompetent. Oh, we've made some good decisions concerning species management and extinction. I'm comforted by that thought that the sabre-toothed tiger is extinct and I needn't be on the lookout for them while guarding a runway near my deer stand. Periodically, too, we arrange a war to help resolve the human overpopulation problem.

But we've also made some frightful errors. Our ancestors sat on their hands and watched a fine game bird like the passenger pigeon get a disease and become extinct. However, neither our progenitors nor any of us have taken serious steps to eradicate such universally recognized pests as woodticks, mosquitoes or politicians. Such oversights are inexcusable.

We can't do much about what has already joined the list of extinct species and there may be, already in motion, irreversible forces which will erase other forms of life from our rolls of flora and fauna. Nevertheless, we should all take a special interest in species which are endangered, supporting efforts to keep those worth saving and helping to nudge those which are now (like the smallpox virus) over the ledge.

If we are to properly assume our responsibilities to maintain the conditions and habitat which are necessary to the continuation of the worthwhile forms of life, it is essential we have accurate information on just what is endangered and what is not.

The people in charge of the Endangered Species List are only human. They are susceptible to blunder and error. We all should help them keep their lists up to date and, as occasion arises, give them helpful suggestions. But such is not an easy task, comrades.

When I reviewed the list of endangered species, one sin of omission fairly leaped from the page. So I called the Audubon Society to enlist their support in expanding the list to include a Hairy Woodpecker. Now, you'd think this kind of public-spirited suggestion would receive a favorable hearing. Well, you had better think again. They rather stuffily informed me the Hairy Wood-pecker was not endangered and claimed there were thousands of breeding pairs.

I kept my temper and calmly told them about the particular Hairy Woodpecker that insists upon banging away at the tin on the chimney of my cabin – at 6 a.m. – throughout the entire summer. I explained that this Hairy Woodpecker was indeed endangered and, as a matter of fact, if it hung around long enough for me to get out of bed, load the .410 and get onto the back porch, it would no longer be endangered. They would be able to transfer him over to the "extinct" list.

And I explained how I thought it was the obligation of any conscientious outdoors-type person to give such birds formal warnings of their jeopardy by putting them on the Endangered Species List. The gentleman on the phone didn't appear to be listening. He just kept repeating: "It isn't endangered. It isn't endangered." He became hysterical and hung up on me. Imagine.

When people in charge display such an obvious and almost pathological estrangement from logic and clear thinking and flatly refuse to consider well-founded suggestions from us folks in the field, then one can only wonder about the reliability of their other work. So, I got copies of the lists of extinct species and of endangered and unendangered species. They, too, contain patent mistakes. Normally I wouldn't want to tell on them, but they've got me mad, so they'll simply have to face the music. Friends, none of their lists – extinct, endangered or unendangered – contains the name of the Woose Grock!

So I called the gentleman again. He remembered me. When confronted with this listing oversight, he resorted to an obvious subterfuge by denying the existence of the bird. He apparently adopted this bizarre posture on the basis of the transparent excuse that he had never touched, smelled, heard, tasted or even seen one – dead, alive, stuffed or in a clear photograph. One might use that same sort of nonsensical and circumstantial argument to disprove the existence of hangovers (and I have it on very good authority that they most certainly do exist).

The Woose Grock does not fly backwards – as is suggested by some of the commentators. The reason for such a misconception is quite simple. You see, the bird's tail is attached to its body at the place where the head would normally be placed. And the head is located on that part of the anatomy which usually houses the tail. The bird's feet are reversed, the back toes pointing forward.

The Woose Grock's said anatomical eccentricities explain why it has never been photographed. When this shy, non-photogenic,

— Sandy Klein Stevens

privacy-loving bird is disturbed and flies away from the flusher, it is looking backwards at its pursuers and can easily dodge and fly behind trees whenever a camera is pointed at it.

And this same uncommon physical structure also explains why no specimen has been taken by hunters or mounted. With the bird's head pointed towards the rear, hunters invariably will lead it in the wrong direction, swinging the barrel 180 degrees from its line of flight and, thus, constantly shoot far behind it.

With no normal hunting pressures, the Woose Grock is not only not extinct, it is not endangered either. It has proliferated, is found abundantly throughout upland game country, and should appear on the Unendangered Species List.

Still, the Woose Grock is not commonly recognized by those unfamiliar with its peculiarities. This is because the male bird looks quite like the ruffed grouse and the female is practically indistinguishable from the woodcock.

Curiously enough, I've never seen a Woose Grock, although I spend most fall weekends wandering around in its favorite kind of habitat. I know they exist because of reports I've received from no less an authority than Chuck Petrie. And Chuck's honesty has never been questioned. (Come to think about it, I've never even heard it mentioned.)

I was hunting with Chuck up in Forest County a few years ago. Chuck saw eleven Woose Grock in a single day. I mistakenly thought he had been firing at (and missing) the abundant ruffed grouse and woodcock, but he explained that they were Woose Grock and, as is consistently the case with those fowl, since their heads are on backwards, he had been leading them in the wrong direction.

≈

John Beth lives in Reedsburg with his wife, Randine, son Damion and daughter Kjersti. He has worked in the music business as a technician, salesperson and musician for over 20 years. A freelance outdoor writer and photographer whose work has appeared in many regional and national publications, he also composes and performs music for outdoor films. Beth is a popular speaker on the subject of fly fishing and is a member of Trout Unlimited and the Federation of Fly Fishers. Although largely a Wisconsin opportunity promoter, he frequents the rivers of Montana and Wyoming as time allows.

Indian Summer Salmon
by
John Beth

My old Buick inched off the pavement onto a patch of worn earth next to the railroad tracks. With half an hour to wait until sunrise, I elected to stretch and have some coffee. The four-hour drive from home to the river had been filled with hopes of finding fall chinook salmon in the river.

"No rush," I said to myself. "No one is here. No one ever is this early in the morning, this late in the year." As I slid into my vest and boots I noticed frost on the tracks, a reminder of November, now only two days away. The steam from my last drink of coffee rose to meet that from my nostrils. Twenty, twenty-five degrees, I thought. Forty by midday, most likely.

I walked briskly down the tracks until I heard rapids ahead. Soon the river, still moonlit, was in sight. I crunched through the frozen grass and eased down the high bank. The 40-degree water sent ghostly swirls of mist into the calm air above the rapids, now backlighted in grey and pink hues on the eastern horizon. I hoped that, as in past years, the big pool ahead would hold some fall kings who would be willing to test my fly tackle in these early dawn hours.

A loud burst of rhythmic splashes surprised me. From the far side of the river came the telltale sound of a big salmon running the rapids. It slowly finned its tail as it rested in the eddy it had just reached. "Big fish," I said aloud. Even though the salmon wasn't quite visible, the wake it had pushed across the pool was still lapping on the boulders at my feet.

I crossed well below the bend pool and cut across an island to try to enter on the upstream side of the pool unnoticed. On the trip through the tall grass I heard two more tail-walks, even above the sounds of vegetation crunching underfoot and the tumbling of the rapids. Emerging at the edge of the river, I crouched to watch four separate wakes working its flatness. Hints of sunlight began to filter through the trees and onto the water.

I'll wait here, I thought. It's a little too dark to make it all out.

No matter how many years I've fished for river salmon, these moments of waiting are still rife with anticipation. If ever ten minutes seemed like an hour, it is the times I've spent preparing for that first cast. I waited, watching the moving silhouettes and tying a number two Kewaunee Autumn fly on my tippet. Finally ready, I knocked loose the last embers from my pipe on my boot heel and began to strip out flyline.

There were at least four big salmon working the water, and the light now exposed a large king at the tail of the bend pond, hovering above the lower rapids. "Forty-inch fish, I'll bet."

The new dawn revealed several other kings in front of me, but my eyes quickly rolled back to the big male below, swimming in slow, wide circles. Suddenly, a burst of water sprayed from the rapids downstream as a large female glided into view. My fish, the male, immediately circled, swam along her side and stopped. In an instant, a smaller male appeared and showed a marked interest in the new girl in town. The brawny fish at her side exploded in a violent lunge toward the intruder. A snap to the head and side of the smaller male made it clear whose lady this was, and a final ten-foot lurch at the fleeing fish's tail should have removed any remaining doubt.

One by one, three other males challenged my king. One by one, he fought them off and circled back to his partner. She, never moving from her protected position, could not have found a more chivalrous mate.

"In the next fight," I muttered under my breath, "there's going to be one more contestant."

Two more invaders from the pool began circling the big male fish, their displays of aggression easily masking my fly as it dropped in the clear water ten feet above them and slowly drifted straight into the scene of battle.

One of the smaller kings shot down the rapids, below the waiting female. The other was giving my king, this time, an earnest fight. I swam the fly quickly by the battling males and lifted it out of the water. The thrashing fish had stirred up the bottom, and I didn't want to risk foul-hooking one of the salmon.

I cast again when the challenging male departed. The fly drifted into the dominant king's field of vision as I twitched the feathered lure toward his lady. He intercepted the animated pest about one foot away from her. As I lifted the rod skyward, the big male immediately rocketed upstream, the streamer's barbless hook buried deep in the hinge of his jaw.

Angry and startled, the salmon shook his head left, then right, in swift, powerful surges, pounding the surface of the pool with his immense tail each time he flexed, then swam on his side against the rocks, twisting my line in his dogged attempts to dislodge the annoying fly.

I kept steady pressure on the fish as he moved to the chest-deep water above me, and could feel him gain power in its depth. I had no choice but to try to head him off from a potential downstream run. There were five miles of river between me and Lake Michigan, and I had only 100 yards of backing on my reel. Increasing line pressure on the king didn't move him. The brute, facing upstream in the deep water ahead of me, almost seemed to be resting.

Suddenly the king turned and raced downstream. He came to the surface as he lunged past, spraying me in the process. In seconds I felt the knot connecting my flyline to the backing bump through my woolen gloves. Stumbling and slipping along the edge of the river, I tried to get line back onto the reel.

Recovering line as I moved downstream with the fish, I regained control of the contest, too. After two more tiring downstream runs, I felt the salmon's strength begin to wane. After a final, dispirited lunge, he conceded.

Though the salmon was now exhausted, attached to the end of my line, I felt humbled by his power and persistence, and his will to be free. As I played him to my feet, the great fish finned slowly in the calm eddy of the railroad pool. I slipped my hand around the thick muscle above his tail and lifted his glistening body high into the clear morning sunlight. The bronze-colored fish, easily forty inches long, dripped river water and snapped his huge, sharp teeth as I wrestled the fly from his jaw. When I looked down I saw both our reflections in the river. I walked out to the edge of the current, salmon in tow.

Stooping to lay the salmon in a shallow run, I saw his eye instinctively roll toward the water as the dry leaves of autumn eddied around him. This great fish would soon spawn and die, predestined, mysteriously, as would all of the river's salmon. Somewhere downstream his bones would bleach on a shallow riffle in December, other animals having feasted on his flesh, drawing life from the king salmon's death.

I held the fish below the surface to keep him stable in the current. Within five minutes his strength was building again and I could feel him once more asking for freedom. This time no hook and line would slow him. "You'll die soon," I said, "but not here, and not today."

Fifty yards upstream his female would be drifting back to the redd. Their spawn would not hatch and give new salmon to the

– Jim Goetz

river, but only I knew that. The big male swam away, slowly, regaining power necessary for the run through the rapids and to once again join his mate. He was gone, but the best part of him remained in my heart and memory. I contemplated his final, sad expression before he returned to his river, his home, his grave. He knew.

I walked the river slowly that day. Corn shocks and pumpkins decorated the distant fields. The brilliant foliage was almost gone from the trees on the hillside; a few faded apples clung to branches of trees along the valley. Silk cobwebs glistened in the clear Indian summer sky and, although the last frost had taken most of the insects, midges still danced in the sunlight in sheltered corners of the river. Fallen leaves canoed the sparkling riffles, and milkweed and thistledown drifted in updrafts over the river like giant snowflakes dancing in the last golden days of autumn.

My day on the river, as always, was too short. As I climbed the bank to leave I looked back over the big bend pool by the railroad tracks where the morning had started. Two long, dark shapes held at the tail of the pool. Then, a flash of silver—the female salmon digging her redd. Her male stayed at her side, guarding her with what was left of his life.

Following my lengthening shadow toward the car, I pondered the mysterious forces that bring salmon, and me, to rivers. For my part, I know, I come not to experience the salmons' deaths but to celebrate their lives – and attempt to understand a bit more of mine.

る

Born in Superior at the extreme western end of "the greatest of the Great Lakes," Roger Drayna grew up in an outdoor family. He sold his first outdoor article in 1951 while in his junior year at the University of Wisconsin-Superior. He has been an avocational freelance writer ever since.

Following a tour of air force duty, he was a professional educator for fourteen years, all of it in Antigo. In 1968 he left teaching to become a writer in the public relations department of the Wausau Insurance Companies and became manager of the department four years later, a position he held until his retirement in June 1992.

Among his writing credits, Drayna lists Sports Illustrated, Sports Afield, Outdoor Life, and the Catholic Digest. His byline is seen most frequently in Wisconsin Trails, where he has been a contributor since 1972. His 150 published pieces also have been in numerous smaller publications.

During his college and teaching years, he worked ten summers for the U. S. Forest Service and the National Park Service. This extensive field experience, he says, has directed him into writing that is nature-interpretive. His favorite outdoor activities are canoeing, canoe camping, and cross-country skiing. He lives in Wausau but is frequently found at his one-room cabin set atop a glacial moraine on forty acres in the Harrison Hills of Lincoln County.

Roger and Marcy Drayna, married 40 years ago, have four grown children, all of whom play roles in his evocative essay "John Macko's Gift."

John Macko's Gift
by
Roger Drayna

It was an early morning last October, I think, when I finally decided I'd have to write about the Johnny Macko Oak. The sun had cleared the hardwood ridges that enclose the Wisconsin River as it streams through Wausau on its way to the Mississippi two hundred and fifty miles downstream. In the early light of this splendid autumn day, coffee mug in hand, I stood looking across the deck at the scarlet, frost-rimmed foliage of John's tree. As I watched, a startling blue form hurtled into a spruce down along the lot line.

"*Jay! Jay!*" it shouted. Somewhere up the street came a reply. Moments later a second blue jay flared and alighted, swaying precariously on a slender limb of the mountain ash.

With quick head movements, they satisfied themselves that no dangers lurked and launched themselves on undulating flights to the oak. They were a scant twenty feet away, yet their search for the last of the acorn crop was hidden by the still dense canopy. I could guess at the progress of their investigations, however, because they set the crimson leaves dancing as they bounced from branch to branch.

We've been watching and caring for the Johnny Macko Oak twenty years now, my family and I. In the early years, we'd wrap its fragile stem each autumn to ward off meadow voles and the cotton-tail rabbits drawn into the yard by spillage from the bird feeder. It's a tree now, a good ten inches in diameter and more than thirty-five feet tall. The bark has taken on that leathery toughness of northern red oak and the voles and the rabbits are no longer interested.

Those who know how slowly oaks grow up here at the northern edge of their range will understand that thirty-five feet in twenty years qualifies as spectacular. I suspect the watching and the caring helped a lot.

We got this oak when my daughter was ten. Back then, I was teaching in Antigo, an agricultural community thirty-five miles northeast of here. Deborah had shown an early love for growing things, and we always had a half dozen projects underway in the backyard – potted maples, a couple of small red pines, assorted wild flowers, things like that.

Johnny Macko's yard backed against the north side of ours. A gentle, stocky Slav, he would walk over in the evening and sit on our back steps in the summer twilight and talk about brook trout in the Eau Claire River or the coming of deer season to the aspen and tag alder thickets of the Ackley Swamp. As he was in his sixties and childless, our three kids, Deborah and her younger brothers, were a delight to him.

John was nearing the end of a working lifetime that had begun early. Schooling past the eighth grade had been a luxury few northern Wisconsin families allowed time for back in the nineteen-twenties. When we knew him, he operated heavy equipment for the county highway department.

Right after supper one evening, when the spring sun had driven away the last of the snow but the hardwood buds had not yet swelled, John knocked at the back door. He was just in from work. Sandy hair stuck in tufts from under a well-crushed cap. His face, heavily tanned from years of outdoor work, had a taut chin and strong cheek planes. Deep wrinkles set off the eyes, as much, I think, from smiling as from squinting into the sun. Wide suspenders accentuated an open-at-the-throat chambray shirt and impressively square shoulders.

In his lunch bucket he had this tiny oak, a foot tall perhaps with a stem no thicker than a pencil. He'd been working on a road cut that day and would have had to shear it away with his bulldozer. Good humor spilled from the blue-gray eyes as he held it out to me with tanned, blunt-fingered hands, "I t'ought Debbie might like to grow it."

That was when we assumed stewardship for the small tree we eventually named the Johnny Macko Oak.

It had three years to grow in the rich glacial loam of Langlade County, and then a turn in my own career brought us to Wausau. There was no way the oak could be left behind. Almost three feet tall by then, it made the trip in a rusty-bottomed old water bucket, securely propped up in the back of our station wagon. That bucket would be its home until transplanting season arrived in the fall.

Our new home was your standard three-bedroom ranch on a lot cut from the Bonny Doon Farm, a dairy on the northwest side of town until homes like ours chewed away at it plot by plot.

The new backyard wasn't much right then, just an expanse of scraggly grass turned brown under the July sun, sloping away to ragged pasture, which was about all that remained of the Bonny Doon Farm.

There was no deck on the back of the house when we bought it, nor did we contemplate the possibility of building one. In selecting a new site for the oak, we simply went out in back with a shovel, tried to imagine where it might look good, and dug it in. Happily, and I'm sure that sheer chance had as much to do with it as any silvicultural sense on our part, we must have placed it in one of the all-time good locations for a northern red oak.

In the morning, the house shadowed it and allowed the dew to keep its leaves moist almost until noon. Full sunlight flooded the spot all afternoon. And the slight hill running down to the back line gave it good drainage during the long spring rains. Whatever the combination of circumstances, and good genetics must also have played a role, it didn't take many seasons for us to realize that the little tree was doing splendidly, adding a couple feet of growth each summer and sometimes more than three.

Some years later, the idea for a deck finally struck us. When we staked out the dimensions of the project, it extended to within six feet of the oak, which was now a sturdy sapling ten or twelve feet in height. It was easy to see that we could not have picked a better spot for it as a shade tree.

Along about then John Macko died, not long into retirement, after a life of unrelenting labor. The years have sped along since, but we've thought of him often while watching this oak become a tree.

My little girl is a woman now, living in the southern part of the state. It's no surprise, I suppose, that her apartment is filled with plants and that her first vacation after a year of lawyering was to the rain forest of Olympic National Park. When she gets home on holiday, going out in back to check on this tree is an early order of business.

The older boys are grown, too. They were such incessant climbers when they were little that we really had to lay down the law about trying to shinny up the tree once it was big enough to present a temptation. Another brother, just getting into his teens, has that pleasure now that it has the strength to tolerate it. He likes to vanish into the cool canopy on a summer day to munch apples and read Sherlock Holmes.

So, the seasons have flowed around this tree and all the loving it has known. In the spring, long tendrils of delicate flowers erupt even as the buds end their dormancy. When the leaves unfurl toward the middle of May, they too are flower-like, possessing all the colors of autumn but so much softer spoken.

Each summer, the branches reach farther over the deck, and we congratulate ourselves again for our wisdom in choosing its growing place as we sit, feet propped on the railing, in the late afternoon coolness. Robins like to make their second nests in the safety of the high, strong crotches. When they do, Paul has to postpone his apple eating and book reading sessions until the nestlings are gone.

Every other year or so we get a bumper crop of acorns, which are fully ripened before the onset of the autumn splendor. It's then that the gray squirrels and the blue jays find us. They hide the tough, russet nuts all over the yard and never manage to find all of them again. I do – as little, twin-leaved oaklings peering out of the grass when I'm mowing the next summer. I've transplanted one down by the garden; it can stay there until Deborah has a place for it. Another is thrusting up from the periwinkle at the base of a birch in the front yard. We're letting it grow; the birch has been looking none too healthy the last couple of years. It would be nice, I often think, to move some of them up to our woods in the Harrison Hills.

Even in the bleak northern winter, the Johnny Macko Oak presents us with abundant joys. There are days of thick hoar frost and others when it stands radiant in the ice from a January rain. Chickadees like to take sunflower seeds and work on them against its tough branches. An occasional cardinal waits shyly on a limb, looking cautiously about before descending to the feeder.

It all started as such a small gift, just a simple act of neighborliness. How important it has become. I liked to tell John about his tree when we talked on the phone each Christmas. It outlived him, and it will probably outlive me. There will come a time, I know, when someone else will sit on this deck and watch sunsets through the cool shade of John's oak. There will be other little girls and other tree climbers. They should know that this is not just another tree. They should know about a tiny red oak that sprouted on a hillside near the Wolf River. They should know about all the watching and caring it took for it to become the Johnny Macko Oak.

– Sharon Anderson

Dion Henderson's writing career spanned 48 years before he died on December 8, 1984, six days short of his 63rd birthday. Henderson sold his first short story to a national magazine when he was 14, and he went on to write hundreds of stories and essays for such magazines as Field & Stream, Argosy, The Saturday Evening Post, Playboy, *and* Defenders of Wildlife. *He also wrote eight books.*

Aside from his writing, Henderson was a newsman. He started working for the Associated Press in 1942, and in 1967 became chief of the Milwaukee Bureau, a position he held until his death. He inspired many writers while serving as editor-in-residence at the Marquette University college of journalism.

Henderson was a student of Aldo Leopold, and his later writing mixed the best of his knowledge of the outdoors with deep concern and appreciation for living things.

"There are few people now who lived so close to the land when they grew up," said his son, Bruce Henderson. "There are few people left who feel so personally the harm that people have done to the living things around them."

The Ninety-Ninth Bear
by
Dion Henderson

The heifer was just beyond the clearing, in the cutover. There was another small clearing around the heifer, one that had not been there before the heifer met the bear. The heifer looked as though it had met a locomotive head-on instead of a bear.

On one side of the kill, the little old man wearing corduroy trousers, long wool socks and the jacket from a business suit smiled wryly. He looked at the broken underbrush, the torn earth and at the heifer and said, "Pretty quick now they will send for Rigeaulx."

He said that because he was Rigeaulx, and always when there was an authentic wolf, or a bear that no one could catch, and it became apparent that no one could catch it, then they sent for

Rigeaulx and Rigeaulx caught it.

"Not this year," the little old man said even more wryly to the young man who stood on the other side of the heifer. "They will try once more for him with open sets because they do not believe an old bear can read the signs. They will fail for two reasons, of which the poorer is sufficient: old bears are very good at the signs you must put up around an open set."

He smiled at the young man and came around the heifer's carcass and the two of them started out through the cutover pasture where the ground already was hard and the sky pressed down heavy with snow. It did not look as though he intended to say any more.

"What's the other reason, the good one?" asked the young man.

Rigeaulx smiled, very broadly this time. He wore an old, close-fitting cap and his white hair curled out around the edges, and if it had not been for the visor on the cap he would have looked like a very handsome old monk. He was nearly eighty years old but when he smiled broadly you saw he had splendid teeth.

"You are as ignorant as anybody," he said to the young man. "Maybe more so. But I like you because you are not so stupid about being ignorant."

"Thank you very much." The young man grinned because mostly it was true. "But what is the best reason they will not catch the bear?"

"Because the kill is several days old and the sign is plain up in the mountain ash, where even now he is denned up beneath some deadfall, relaxing in the first delicious stages of the long sleep," Rigeaulx chuckled. "And meanwhile they will drag in the big traps and make the elaborate preparations and put up the large signs and while the bear sleeps they will maybe catch a stray dog."

He winked at the young man. You could tell he winked because while there was not room for any more wrinkles around his eyes, one of them sort of disappeared.

"It is such a terrible thing to catch a partridge hunter in a bear trap," Rigeaulx said. "You can't do much except shoot him, because if you let him out he will chase you clear to Superior."

Despite this, the young man knew Rigeaulx was very serious about the bear. He was a very important bear, because everyone said when he was gone, they would not have to worry about bears anymore. It did not seem possible to the young man that the bear ever would be gone. Of course, he had not been there forever. But there is something about a big bear, that when he is in your country for ten or twelve years it seems like forever. In addition, when the young man first learned of him, the bear already was old and famous, as bears get famous, within the twenty-five or thirty square miles of their range.

That was in early spring, when the young man was passing through the Indianhead country and stopped off just to see how the River of the Braves would look by trout season time. One of the puppies was with him and they walked down from the old bridge across the horseshoe of the Braves and around the bend where the rapid of the long fall begins. There is a marsh meadow there in the spring when the Braves has too much water trying to get through the rapids all at once. There was sign of considerable upheaval in the meadow, among the snow lilies and skunk cabbage, but the young man did not think about bear until he went on to where he could see the trees.

The bear had been working on them, apparently skinning back the bark to get at the cambium layer for some mysterious, medicinal purpose. The marks on the trees were nearly as tall as he was.

Now the men whose experience reaches out to embrace grizzlies and Alaskan browns and such would not be much impressed by this, but the young man's circle of acquaintance among bears was very limited and furthermore was going to stay that way if he had anything to say about it. There is no doubt but what a black bear that skins trees nearly six feet high is a considerable quantity of bear. A black bear not any taller at the shoulder than a bird dog and five feet or so long may weight 400 pounds when meated up, and rumors have come in from far places of blacks twice that heavy. The North American record pelt was seven feet long and eight feet wide.

The young man looked at the skinned trees very thoughtfully and then heard a strangled growl from the puppy. The pup was standing with his outraged nose in a track, every hair aloft and looking generally as no pointer dog should look, but the rage that was in him went back a long time before there were pointer dogs and had to do with ancestral voices.

The track was a good one, in soft mud that had kind of squished out so that it likely was bigger than it should have been but even so it was eight inches or more. It was a forefoot track and showed five toes, which might have meant the bear was running or else that he had no intention whatever of running. Presently the young man called the puppy and when he declined to move the young man picked him up, rigid with indignation, and carried him back to the car.

One other time, in another year, he saw the bear. It was late summer and he was fishing the lower stretch of the Braves, where it has leveled and widens out for a mile and looks as though it might be any fine meadow stream, if you did not know it was the River of the Braves. He was tired and hungry and it had been a fine day and he was just getting ready to leave the gravel riffs reluctantly when he heard the bellow and splashing upstream.

From a knoll nearby he could see the bear. He was a black bulk, thrashing furiously in the shallows. Maybe he had fallen in while berrying; maybe he had been fishing and a fish slipped away and he reacted as a man might. Some bears are as silly about losing their tempers as people are, as many a porcupine could testify. For a little while the young man watched him, then the bear waded out of the water and humped away, head down and swinging, heavy-footed, irritable.

Later the young man wanted to tell Rigeaulx about him. The old man had a house in town, a weathered old house set in two acres of grounds and when you left the street and went through the gate in the hedge you were in the big woods. Rigeaulx said he had worked very hard all his life to keep his place looking as though no one ever had done anything to it. He listened to the anecdote about the bear, then said: "He grows old. Thus it is. When you grow old, the joints stiffen and it is difficult to get around the way you did, and you begin to think of easier ways to make a living." He looked at the young man wryly and said, "I know what I am talking about. The temptation is great."

The young man asked, "Will you have to trap him then?"

"Why should I trap him?" Rigeaulx was partly fooling and partly not fooling. "What do you have when the last bear is gone? And the last wolf?"

"I don't know," the young man said. "What?"

"Why, you have safety; it is safe then to have more farms too poor to support people, and more people who cannot live on the farms and finally you have the tourists who are disappointed because they really came to see bears."

The young man did not say anything and Rigeaulx winked at him.

"Furthermore, you then have unemployed bear trappers who might become a threat to the peace of the community, but they have not thought of that yet and you must not tell them. If the time comes when they must trap Rigeaulx as a predator, I want the surprise to be all on their side."

The young man smiled and Rigeaulx said, "Do not laugh. I am not so young either. There are all kinds of temptations."

But as far as the bear was concerned, he was quite right. That next year the bear came out in the spring and killed a calf in a backwoods pasture, and shortly thereafter a sheep, and a little while after that a whole pasture of sheep, one at a time, until they were all gone.

The next spring everyone who had not tried before had a chance at the bear. They tried trail layouts and the bear went out of his way to find them and scrape them clear and leave the traps naked and wicked-looking unsprung. They tried a bawling calf near his favorite haunts and trapped the approaches and he killed three sheep ten miles away. They erected a set gun in the defile that led to the berrying ground and after three weeks shot the only good Holstein bull in the country. The bear was having a fine time.

At last they came to Rigeaulx.

The young man heard about it as soon as he arrived that year at the cabin on the bank of the Braves. He heard it from Rigeaulx himself. On the first evening he was sitting in the kitchen of the cabin sorting patterns in his fly book when the old man came in and sat down. The coffeepot was full and Rigeaulx brought it to the table with him. There was a comb of honey on a plate and he cut off a slab with his belt knife, put it in a mug and poured the coffee in on top of it, very hot and mixing with the honey to make a hot, sweet smell in the cabin.

"You are just in time to witness the advance of progress," Rigeaulx said, not as cheerfully as usual.

"Progress?"

"That was their very word," said Rigeaulx. "Each of them had an interest in it and used it as though he were its proprietor. 'You got to have progress,' they say to Rigeaulx. But Rigeaulx replies that he does not got to have anything."

"So there was a whole delegation," the young man said.

"Having in common two things," Rigeaulx went on. "Being the word 'progress,' and a mutual inability to dominate this one bear."

The young man did not say anything. He fixed himself a mug of coffee and honey and tasted it warily. It was good.

"I can remember," Rigeaulx said, "when their grandfathers talked similarly of 'progress,' and for the same reason."

"I knew it went back quite a while," the young man said.

"Ninety-eight times," Rigeaulx said. "Ninety-eight bears I have caught for them. One of them was an old sow with young." His old face brightened. "She weighed six hundred pounds and if I had her this minute I would put her in the office of the authorities and lock the door and pretty soon she would weigh a half a ton and then I could catch her again and have simultaneously a world record black bear and no authorities to contend with."

The idea amused him. It amused the young man too, but only until he stopped to consider it. Then he said, "So you are going to catch the bear."

"Sure," Rigeaulx said. "Both the bear and I have lived too long now, we have become too useful. That is a worse thing than out-living your usefulness, which is maybe impossible anyway. Sure, Rigeaulx will catch the bear. If the bear was Rigeaulx, he would catch me. We will understand each other."

"Well," the young man said, "I guess I always knew you would do it. You couldn't stand in the way of progress all by yourself."

"I could stand there indefinitely," Rigeaulx said. "But then they suggested since no one else could catch this bear, perhaps Rigeaulx could not either. Now the bear has to go."

"It was a dirty trick to pull that now," the young man said feelingly.

"Sure," said Rigeaulx. He smiled suddenly. "It was a dirty trick the other ninety-eight times too. Everyone knows that Rigeaulx is very proud. It is a good thing for the bears that Rigeaulx is very patient, but no one knows about that."

The young man did not really understand that part. He was going to question the old man about it, but Rigeaulx was talking about bears and the young man did not want to miss it and in the end he forgot that he did not understand until much later. Instead he asked something foolish about why it was easy for Rigeaulx to catch the bears when the others could not.

"As I said . . ." Rigeaulx fixed himself another mug of coffee, the last in the pot, "you are very ignorant. The others do not understand how you must say to yourself as I do: Rigeaulx, you are a bear, a very bad bear, now what are you going to do? And then I understand what I, Rigeaulx the bear, would do. I circumvent me and put the trap and it is very easy."

Up to a point, the young man followed him.

"There's one thing," he insisted. "Even if you think as the bear, and the bear does, too, why do you not come out even sometimes?"

"Oh," Rigeaulx said with that splendid smile. "It is a matter of experience. I have been a bear much oftener than he has."

Then he said, "The coffee was very good but the honey is the fancy, sweet, clover honey. Weed honey is better."

That was all the talk there was about the bear. Until one night Rigeaulx woke the young man in the cabin. It was still dark and there was a bite in the air. He was wearing the corduroy pants and the wool stockings but he had put on pacs instead of moccasins and he was wearing a gunbelt with his worn old Peacemaker holstered on it.

"I thought maybe you would like to see the bear," he said. "Perhaps you would like to bring a camera."

The young man struggled out of sleep.

"Have you caught him?"

"No." Rigeaulx grinned. "But it will be after sunup when we get to the trap, and he will be in it. Right now he is sitting outside it, meditating."

The young man shuddered a little, but crawled out and dressed while Rigeaulx made the coffee. He had brought some weed honey in the comb with him, and the young man tried it in the coffee. Rigeaulx was right, it was better.

Then the young man had his camera and they were out in the woods and the young man was busy just trying to keep up with the old man's frail little figure, flitting eerily through the cutover where the young man could have gotten hopelessly lost in a dozen square rods. The young man felt himself traveling with all the grace of a five-legged hippopotamus, and was reminded of another alarming thing Rigeaulx once told him. Many hunters are adequate woodsmen, the old man said, but generally the old wardens and enforcement officers are the best, because hunters do not have the same incentive.

Suddenly he stopped. "He is there now," Rigeaulx said. "Do you hear?"

The young man heard nothing but the dying echoes of a deer's flight and the far sound of geese. They went another quarter-mile before he heard.

Up close, it was very bad. The sun was up then, but it was overcast and a drizzle had begun. The bear was making a good deal of noise but the noise he made bellowing was not the worst of it. You could hear the thud of his weight being thrown around, and the crash of the brush and occasionally the pistol-shot sound that was a tree breaking. Then they were near enough to see the vast bulk thrashing around in the popple, indistinct except for the sweeps he made and the red and white explosion that was his mouth snapping blindly at whatever was in the way. He had the trap on one forepaw, well up, and he carried the fifty pounds like it was nothing. Eight feet of heavy chain was on it, and an oak-log drag and when he stood up and roared and swung his forepaws around him in a horrifying gesture of destruction, the chain and the drag log snapped around him like the tail on a storm-carried kite.

The drag log caught on every bit of brush and the bear struggled with it in rage, then would give up and go back and tear it loose and once picked it up almost tenderly for an instant the way you hold a baby. Then he dropped it and rushed furiously away and the log caught between two big poplars and the bear made a soprano sound of almost human intensity and whirled on the trees and took one of them off at a single snap. Afterward, the young man looked and the tree was six inches across.

"Maybe I had better end it now," Rigeaulx said sadly.

"Wait a minute," the young man said. "Let me get some pictures." He was very flushed and exhilarated and did not wait to plan what he was doing. He plunged down into the dense popple in the wake of the bear, and when he thought he was close enough he stopped to adjust the camera. Then the bear turned, raging, to tear loose the drag log one time more and came back for it and saw the young man and kept coming; a huge, clumsy-looking bulk, moving with unbelievable speed and grace across the smashed thicket, and the young man turned frantically but tripped and the bear was very close. The young man was kneeling and held up the camera before him almost in supplication and the bear accepted the sacrifice, making a great taloned slash that sent the camera flying into pieces that the young man saw very sharply and memorably etched against the cold, blue sky in the instant before he scrambled wildly to safety and the bear was caught again by the drag.

Rigeaulx had the old Peacemaker in his hand, but he had been unable to shoot and when the young man plunged feverishly out toward him, he did not have any alarm nor fear nor even mild concern on his face, only his great age and a strange sadness. It was as though there was something here, between him and the bear, that did not leave room for any kind of feelings about ignorant young men.

"Later," he said wryly to the young man, "you will be very interested to read the expert opinions on how a bear will not attack a man unless he is cornered. You may even write some."

"No," the young man said shakily. "I have read them already. But once I met a bear who thought he was cornered every time a man got in the same county with him. This one ought to be absolutely positive."

"There is another possibility, too." Rigeaulx was very casual, as though he were discussing the weather or some other matter that he did not have to think about while talking. "Some bears are very poorly educated and thus do not know what they are supposed to do. I will mention it to the supervisor so that he may take steps with future bears while they are young and eager for knowledge."

He winked at the young man and took the Peacemaker in both old hands, holding it very gently for a moment, then walked casually down into the bewildering maze of black ground and mist and the white bones of popple where the bear waited.

In the middle of the thicket, the stand was very dense and the trees were older. A man had to pick his way carefully, squeezing between some boles. The bear did not have this trouble, by himself. He was very big and very angry and he hurt terribly and he went in a straight line, bending some trees and breaking those that did not bend. The drag log was too much, though, because it was on the ground and caught between the stumps and presently the bear was jammed in tightly, and before he could go back to loosen the log he saw Rigeaulx coming toward him and did not try to go back any more.

He loomed, half standing, between two trees, not making any noise now but panting a little, and Rigeaulx walked up to him very calmly and looked at the bear and the bear looked at him and very swiftly and skillfully Rigeaulx put the .44 up against the bear's ear and shot him. The bear looked at him a few seconds more, still without making any noise, then lay down very carefully and died.

The young man went back to the set to see how Rigeaulx had done so easily what no one else could do. There was a huge, white pine stump, remnant of an old burn, standing seven or eight feet high and burned out inside. There was a slot in one side of it like a gate, but too narrow for a man or a bear to get through without squeezing. Inside the stump, Rigeaulx had hung a tin can full of honey from a bar across the top, with the bottom of the can punctured so the honey dripped out and fell in a little pool at the bottom of the hollow, where the trap had been set.

"It does not look any different to me," the young man said. "But they have tried that kind of a set on him before. On one of them he just pulled the trap out and sprung it and on the other he took the stump apart from the other side."

"They do not understand such bears," Rigeaulx said. "They left the slot plainly as the place where they wanted him to go in and he did not like it, he was old and crotchety and he knew there was no good in doing what men wanted him to do so he would not go in. All I did was make him think he was being kept out."

The young man looked. Rigeaulx had fastened a flimsy, two-inch sapling across the slot in the stump, about a foot high, and the bear had torn it away contemptuously and put his foot down where it had been, and where it had been was where the trap waited.

"I had the advantage," Rigeaulx said. "In my time, I have seen some very smart bears."

After a while, Rigeaulx said, "It is all right. He will leave a fair pelt behind him as a memorial. I did not make any holes in it."

Then they started back to town for help. Rigeaulx said the bear would weigh more than five hundred pounds. Once they stopped so the young man could get his breath.

"Ninety-nine bears," Rigeaulx said.

Suddenly the young man looked almost normal. Ninety-nine and that would be all. No more bears. There would be no presence in the woods to make you remember your hereditary fears. Something would be gone and the woods would be forever changed: safe for livestock and tranquil for picnics and somehow incomplete but full of disturbing recollections, like an abandoned cemetery.

"Rigeaulx," the young man said. "Why did you do it? Why did you catch the last bear for them?"

The little old man looked at him sharply, then looked away and instead of being regretful, he chuckled.

"They asked me, too," he said. "And I did not tell them. But I told you, and although I told you, you still do not know. You are truly an ignorant young man."

"Wait a minute," the young man said eagerly. "You said you were

— Paul Birling

very patient."

"Yes, indeed," Rigeaulx said. "Very patient, indeed. I had to wait for him to go a-courting, and to marry, and to raise up for himself a family. For a time I was afraid he would be a bachelor bear, and then I should have been very desperate."

The young man stared.

"Still," Rigeaulx said, "I will not tell anyone, and it may be some time after the rejoicing over the last bear has died down before someone comes upon the footsigns of the new sow and the two yearling cubs. Everyone will be happy for quite a while." Then he added, wryly as ever, "but in another five or maybe even ten years they will come to Rigeaulx and they will plead that there is a very bad old bear and I will go out and catch number one hundred, but even that will not be the end of anything."

"Then what?" asked the young man.

"Then maybe I will live forever," Rigeaulx said. "Who wants to catch more than one hundred bears?"

The young man was rested and they continued back to town. Once there was a strange rustle and thumping some distance to one side and the young man jumped a little, then grinned to himself. The woods would be all right for quite a while yet.

&

During his more than four decades as a writer, Don L. Johnson has taken his readers on outdoor adventures to some of the most remote regions of the world. However, the woods and waters of his native Wisconsin have been the scenes of much of his best work.

His byline has appeared in a wide range of publications and he has won honors from a long list of professional and conservation organizations. He received the Gordon MacQuarrie Foundation Medal in 1960, was named an honorary life member by the Wisconsin Outdoor Communicators Association in 1990, and was inducted into the Media Hall of Fame by the Milwaukee Press Club in 1991.

Johnson was the outdoor columnist for the Eau Claire Leader-Telegram for 11 years before moving to the Milwaukee Sentinel's outdoor desk in 1962. He left to become a full-time freelancer in 1985. He is editor-at-large of Wisconsin Outdoor Journal, and his writing appears in that and other magazines.

Although fond of all outdoor sports, Johnson describes his favorite pastimes as "fooling around with dogs, gunning for grouse and woodcock, and flyfishing for trout or panfish." He and his wife, Lorraine, now live in Menomonie. A daughter lives in Medford and a son lives in the state of Maryland, where there also are four grandchildren – "regretfully too far away to be properly spoiled by grandma and indoctrinated into a slothful lifestyle by grandpa."

Memories
by
Don L. Johnson

In the old basswood tree just outside the cabin, a barred owl blinked and bid goodbye to a starry night: "Hoot-hoot, hoot HOOT owl-l-l-l-r-r-r." I could almost hear a yawn at the end.

The cabin was dark, cold, quiet. Now was the time when I should hear Chips padding over to my bunk to nudge my cheek with a cold nose, reminding me of appointments and promises. Grouse season had begun that way for eleven autumns. How swiftly those years had passed. And now my old springer spaniel sidekick was gone. I huddled a bit deeper into the sleeping bag and let my mind travel back through time.

Was it really 14 years since I'd rested on a windswept ridge and watched a big, handsome springer spaniel boldly quartering through the Aleutian tundra below us?

"We don't see such husky springers afield back home anymore," I'd remarked to my companion Bob Mitchell. "He reminds me of how hunting spaniels looked when I was a kid."

Mitchell grinned proudly. A chief petty officer, he was the U.S. Navy's conservation officer on the island of Adak – a rugged piece of real estate jutting from frigid seas far from Alaska's mainland. His dog, Squire, a solid 55 pounds of enthusiasm, was well-bred for hunting ptarmigan in tough terrain and fetching waterfowl from icy waters.

Inevitably, sometime during a memorable week of hunting and fishing, I'd mentioned that I'd like to have a dog like that.

A call came from Mitchell a couple of years later. Retired from the Navy and settled in Wisconsin, he had just become the owner of a lively litter of puppies, sired, of course, by Squire.

"There's a big, bold male that's got your name on him," I was told.

That was in December. Chips came to live with us as soon as he was weaned and he soon proved to be the most precocious pup I'd ever trained. Almost as soon as he could stand on wobbly legs, he began retrieving a glove tossed across the kitchen floor. By April I had a bird dog.

Starlings were raiding the backyard bird feeder *en masse* that winter and I began ambushing them with a pellet rifle from a garage window. The fuzzy, liver-and-white pup caught onto the game almost immediately. He would wait patiently with me in the chilly garage until he heard the pop of the gun, then charge out the door and bound through the snow to fetch the fallen bird. Before spring arrived he had neatly retrieved nearly forty starlings, including some which had required spirited chases or painstaking tracking through the woods behind the house.

I was jolted from reverie when my bare feet hit the ice-cold linoleum as I rolled from the bunk. I groped for a match. The gas light sputtered, then glowed. The morning routines were performed quickly, mechanically. The coffee kettle was steaming as I pulled on my boots. But however much I hurried, Chips would have been whining softly, reminding me that autumn days are always too short for all there is to do. I smiled, remembering how that stubby tail would blur as we headed for the door. It seemed to vibrate until the tail was wagging the dog.

The truck was shrouded with frost, cold as a coffin, but it grumbled and growled to life at the first turn of the key. I went through a mental checklist as the wipers rasped at the windshield:

Gun, shells, compass, knife, thermos, snacks. Everything I needed for the morning's hunt, except for one thing. I slipped the whistle lanyard around my neck. There was no dog to heed my signals today, but I would wear it in memory of a friend.

The memories were keen as I drove down familiar backroads, coarse gravel crunching under the wheels. Good old happy-go-lucky Chips. He had met every day with joy and my every whim with enthusiasm. He was intensely interested in all kinds of fishing, even when it meant keeping long vigils at a hole in the ice. He had logged countless miles in the bow of my canoe, and on backpacking treks he had cheerfully carried his own load in a saddlebag-type pack.

Chips had enjoyed foraging too. While I filled a pail with blackberries, Chips would snuffle up overripe fruit which had fallen to the ground or even nip berries from the prickly canes. He also became expert at finding wild asparagus. The trouble was I had to get there before he'd chomped every stalk to the ground. He had developed a passion for the stuff.

Yes, Chips had indeed been a dog for all seasons. We had spent many memorable days afield for pheasants; had shared waterfowl blinds in every kind of weather. But his biggest passion, from puppyhood to old age, had been our quests for woodcock and grouse, and our favorite coverts were just ahead.

The sun was topping the trees. It was going to be one of those mint-scented mornings when there are torch parades in the maples; when sunbeams dance in the aspens. Frost-nipped bouquets of goldenrod and blue asters still nodded along the roadside. The fireweeds had gone to seed, their airy plumes waving where two deer posed in a clearing, russet summer coats suddenly turned to winter gray.

Wisps of cold mist still swirled up from the creek as I rumbled across an old bridge, parked, and studied the terrain. It was a place where woodcock always waited early in the season. However, the alders, still densely green, seemed taller than I remembered. The creek was high too, thanks to recent rains.

I recalled one opening weekend when the water was much lower. Wearing hipboots, I'd simply waded slowly upstream while Chips worked through the alders on first one side, then the other. I remembered the merry tinkle of his bell, the twittering wings as woodcock fluttered into view; the exaggerated pride with which Chips made each retrieve.

Now, alone in one of our favorite old haunts, I tried to swallow the lump in my throat and headed into the cover. The alders showered me with melting frost. Sometimes they formed a tangle which forced me to back off and try a different tack. When branches snatched my cap, I recalled the words of Harry Croy, one of my old grouse hunting mentors. "If the brush takes your cap off, you're hunting too fast."

I stopped often. It's a thing a dogless hunter has to remember. A halt unnerves tight-sitting birds and they'll often take wing, thinking they've been seen. A hunter who knows good cover and the right technique can take grouse and woodcock quite often without canine assistance. However, I'd rather share any kind of a hunt with a good dog than to bag a limit without one.

I paused, expectant, at a bend in the stream. How many times had I waited for Chips to quarter through that opening ahead? I imagined I could hear his bell above the tinkling current of the creek. I thought I could see him ghosting through the alders. Then a woodcock rose nearby, flew off on tipsy wings and fluttered down again across the creek.

The bird, at least, had been real. But I hadn't been able to shoot. Tears blurred my eyes. I headed back to the truck, picking up my cap several times along the way. I had learned that I could not hunt the old familiar covers. Not yet. Perhaps not until an eager pup earned the right to wear Chips' bell.

Gloomily, I took a circuitous route back to the cabin. Along the way, a weathered "For Sale" sign invited exploration down an overgrown trail into unfamiliar territory. Here perhaps the ghost of Chips might stay at heel for a time. The first quarter-mile was wet going, frogs catapulting across puddles as I slogged along. Here and there, red holly berries gleamed from the trail's edge, reminding me of a favorite Owen Gromme grouse painting.

Near the edge of a beaver pond I found the fresh spoor of a bear. While poking along in search of more tracks in the mud, I jumped a pair of mallards from the flowage. I watched over the barrels of my gun as they disappeared. Duck season was not yet open, but even if it had been, I had the wrong ammunition.

The first grouse flushed unseen, a muffled blur of sound, as I worked along the edge of the alders. It was nearly half an hour before I heard another, clucking nervously on the ground. The foliage was so dense that I could barely see the bird, though it was only 20 feet away. I took another step, tensed for the flush. The grouse vanished with its first wingbeat. I lowered the gun, still unfired for the season, and resignedly began the trek back to the road.

I wasn't prepared for the grouse which burst out of the alders 10 minutes later, but a grouse hunter relies a lot on reflexes. The 20-gauge double came up and fired. A splash told that the bird had fallen into the beaver pond. I ached for Old Chips anew as I waded waist-deep into icy water to fetch my prize.

It was a young bird. An encouraging sign. There are lean autumns for grouse hunters when brood survival has been poor. Another bird was heard flying off through the greenery as I sloshed back to the truck, but I didn't follow. The day had grown warm. Mosquitoes whined. Bees buzzed in the frost-nipped goldenrods.

Back at the cabin, I changed to dry clothes and hungrily envisioned dinner as I lit the oven on the propane stove and set it to 500 degrees. The field-dressed grouse was skinned and a big dollop of margarine was placed into its body cavity. I'd have used butter if I'd had it. A generous sprinkling of black pepper and a couple of shakes of salt followed the margarine. Then the bird was tightly wrapped in a couple thicknesses of aluminum foil, taking care that there were no punctures. Thirty minutes in the oven completed the transformation of a bedraggled-looking grouse into a tender, succulent feast.

Eagerly, I dabbed a slice of bread into the rich gravy and carved steaming white meat from the breastbone. But it wasn't as savory as anticipated. There was something lacking. I knew that it was the nudge of a cold nose to remind me that the neck and giblets are a good bird dog's due.

I changed my mind about staying another day. Almost mechanically, I set the mousetraps, did the dishes, swept the floor. My footsteps echoed behind me as I headed out the door. The cabin had never seemed so empty. Nor had my heart.

❧

– Sandy Klein Stevens

John Bates works as a teacher, naturalist, and writer in northern Wisconsin. His greatest interest is simply exploring the northwoods with his family. Bates lives near Mercer, on the edge of the Manitowish River Wilderness Area and spends "an inordinate amount of time poking around "'cross river." His column "Northwoods Almanac" appears biweekly in The Lakeland Times, Minocqua, and his poetry and articles have appeared in a variety of publications.

Plunkett Road
by
John Bates

I am drawn to roads that appear to start nowhere and go nowhere, roads whose purpose is remembered only in a few elderly hearts and minds, and then rather dimly. The Northwoods, like any rural place, is home to many of these once-vital highways. The value of each may have been as small as providing access to one homesteader's cabin, or as large as carrying traffic to a whole region.

These roads could of course tell stories, if the crumbling asphalt had such an inclination. Part of the pleasure in walking them today is in trying to read the intentions and dreams of those who used them. Once arteries in people's lives, they have been reduced to the smallest capillaries. But that only serves to intensify the exploratory questions that arise on a quiet, early morning hike.

Plunkett Road is such a road, just a mile south of the tiny crossroads of Manitowish. The one that's left today runs just under a mile, a small cutoff segment of what was once Highway 51. Only blackberry pickers and grouse hunters use it now, and then only in season. The old lane sprouts alder and willow, and the asphalt is heaved up in hummocks, bursting the roadway in slow, concentrated earthquakes. Here geology comes alive as hard rock and tar evolve into soft green.

Old Highway 51 once carried the trade and tourists of the North along this section, until engineers felt compelled to straighten the curves and increase the speed of entry into the north country. My father-in-law laughs about the first roads he drove on to reach Manitowish, where his wife was raised. "The roads followed the contours of the land," he says, shaking his head. "Never could get over 35 miles per hour."

In those days, you did not travel north and back in a weekend rush. You came and stayed a while. The roads allowed few other options, respecting land ownership, bowing to nature's eccentric formation of bogs and highland, rolling and curving, free from the modern slavery to speed.

The Plunkett family homesteaded back off the road before the first asphalt was laid, before the first yellow line was drawn. Their life has no remarkable twists to it, but as with everyone who struggled to plow ground and find a living in an area where nothing was easy, it is remarkable just in itself. Only the barest pieces of their story remain. Jim Plunkett logged in the area in the late 1800s, probably as a jobber for the Chippewa Lumber and Boom Company. As all loggers did in those times, he had his own log marking hammer. His mark, *YPJ*, was registered February 3, 1892.

Mrs. Plunkett moved from Eau Claire to the homestead at the turn of the century and was famous later in her life for requiring visitors to come in and have tea, whether they wished to or not. Her home was the only one along that stretch of road, and there may as well have been a barricade stopping travelers in front of her house. To pass by without stopping just wasn't neighborly.

Her three boys, Bill, Jim, and Matt, remained at the homestead after she died. Bill and Jim were bachelors, spending their lives on the homestead, leaving no heirs. The house lacked polish after the mother died in the early thirties. One gentleman has written to me to describe the inside of the house: "The partitions had never been finished to define the various rooms, and the paint to protect it was purchased, but remained in the cans."

Bill carved out a little farm along the river, had cows and horses and a big garden, and plowed for those who wouldn't or couldn't. He was a small Irishman with a squeaky, high voice that rambled too fast. Later in his life a friend described him as having pure white hair and flashing blue eyes, looking as Santa Claus might during his 11-month off-season.

Matt, the third son, bought a cabin on a point of tall pines along the river a few hundred yards from the homestead and rented it to tourists. Matt eventually married and moved to the town of Manitowish, but had no children.

Today the foundation of Matt's cabin sinks slowly into the sandy soil. The old white pines encircle the remains, and eagles hunt from branches that arch out toward the river. Snakes hide in the rotted wood and rock foundation rubble. Otters enjoy dinners under the pines – crayfish-impregnated droppings under one particular pine attest to their presence.

Precious little else is known about the Plunketts. Why would they leave such a beautiful spot to no one, and why would no relations arise to take the land and work with it again? That is all part of the intrigue of Plunkett Road.

Highway 51, in its present form, was straightened and rerouted in the early 1950s. Today Plunkett Road is roughly a half-circle, entering and exiting directly onto Highway 51, with street signs at either end that are impossible for motorists speeding by at 55 mph to read.

A tangled cedar swamp lies between Matt's cabin and another highland of pines, which were recently logged. Rows of scotch pines, planted by the DNR in the 1960s, stand at an even height near the homestead. A little dirt lane leads into the homestead, and the land is still open, as if the forces of old field succession have held off to honor the spot. The skeleton of a massive willow rises below the home site, providing pileated woodpeckers the raw material for sculpting future nest cavities. Along the bank of the river are old bottles and cans, the bachelors having deposited their garbage, as was the custom of the time, by throwing it over the hill leading down to the river.

The river, too, has changed. The main channel once flowed along the length of the homestead, but its course has shifted away from the road. Now a slough calmly rests here, a safe haven for wood ducks and muskrat and painted turtles. A beaver lodge sprawls in the shallows, and the skinned, pale white branches of aspen and alder, which once made up the beaver's winter cache, bob along the banks.

Both the road and river are backwaters now; they've lost their flow of traffic but gained other lives in the loss. The process of change has reshaped this spot in the thousands of years since the glacier's retreat. That this land is again reverting to a wild state is certain, and for me, a gain.

An eagle's nest across the river from the slough first drew me here 12 years ago. I have watched the nest every spring since then. Three years ago it was gone, apparently blown down in a winter storm. I searched the big pines up and down the river, and within two weeks found a new nest coarsely woven in a tall pine several hundred yards upriver from the blowdown.

The spring of 1991 was the first that no eagles nested across from the Plunkett homestead. Loggers were back along Matt's point harvesting wood, but staying the required quarter mile away from the nest. The sights and sounds of logging across the river and marsh leading to the nest must have been too much for the eagles, however. Possibly they nested elsewhere.

Other wildlife, though, have adopted the area. Kestrels perch on the old telephone wires to hunt the roadside ditches and weedy fields, which harbor meals of mice and insects. Grouse flush from the young aspen, the new pioneers of the land near Matt's cabin. Red fox dens are hollowed into the hillside sand rising from the river.

The land is healing. One lane of the road is nearly indistinguish-able from the ditches, and where the healing is slower the road is gently breaking up in chunks. In late April, wood frogs and spring peepers chorus from the wetlands along the road, and migrating ducks rest in the slough. By early summer, purple knapweed, mullein, and sweet fern push up through the broken blacktop, and the road smells curiously of hot asphalt and humus. By early August, blackberry canes laden with fruit lean over the decaying road edge, and the river is often so slow that canoeists scrape the sandy bottom as they pass by the homestead.

Walking this road gives me an understanding of place and order, of time and hope. I see tiny seedlings that withstood years of darkness and crushing weight germinate and gradually burst through the black asphalt mass. Over time, the plants' powers are imposing, yet, in an instant, their strength can't be felt against the hand. Physical law would seem to say such small lives could not push through tar and rock. But growth and reclamation go on every day here, without fanfare or machinery or sweat. The inexorable drive, the life force, even in the small mosses, is Herculean.

Each time I walk Plunkett Road I am inspired. I take home with me the resolve, the prayer to be as strong as the emerging plants and mosses, knowing if I find such strength of will, I too may have breakthroughs in places I thought beyond my reach.

– Sandy Klein Stevens

Aldo Leopold (1887-1948)was one of Wisconsin's best-known writers. He opened his visionary world of conservation ethics and philosophy to us in his monumental A Sand County Almanac. A pioneer in the fields of ecology and wildlife management, and the first to hold the chair of the department of wildlife management at the University of Wisconsin, Leopold opened the eyes of the world to the sensitive and delicate balance of the natural world.

Honored for his accomplishments during his lifetime and beyond, Leopold's principles and philosophies continue to be the foundation of environmental teaching around the world. He was a man of vision. And it was, perhaps, the quiet times out at "The Shack" on his Adams County farm that helped him to see these visions in their clearest form. Here are a few moments from the autumn season in central Wisconsin from the pages of A Sand County Almanac.

Smoky Gold/Red Lanterns
by
Aldo Leopold

There are two kinds of hunting: ordinary hunting and ruffed-grouse hunting.

There are two places to hunt grouse: ordinary places, and Adams County.

There are two times to hunt in Adams: ordinary times, and when the tamaracks are smoky gold. This is written for those luckless ones who have never stood, gun empty and mouth agape, to watch the golden needles come sifting down, while the feathery rocket that knocked them off sails unscathed into the jackpines.

The tamaracks change from green to yellow when the first frosts have brought woodcock, fox sparrows, and juncos out of the north. Troops of robins are stripping the last white berries from the dogwood thickets, leaving the empty stems as a pink haze against the hill. The creekside alders have shed their leaves, exposing here and there an eyeful of holly. Brambles are aglow, lighting your footstep grouseward.

The dog knows what is grouseward better than you do. You will do well to follow him closely, reading from the cock of his ears the story the breeze is telling. When at last he stops stock-still, and says with a sideward glance, 'Well, get ready,' the question is, ready for what? A twittering woodcock, or the rising roar of a grouse, or perhaps only a rabbit? In this moment of uncertainty is condensed much of the virtue of grouse hunting. He who must know what to get ready for should go and hunt pheasants.

Hunts differ in flavor, but the reasons are subtle. The sweetest hunts are stolen. To steal a hunt, either go far into the wilderness where no one has been, or else find some undiscovered place under everybody's nose.

Few hunters know that grouse exist in Adams County, for when they drive through it, they see only a waste of jackpines and scrub oaks. This is because the highway intersects a series of west-running creeks, each of which heads in a swamp, but drops to the river through dry sand-barrens. Naturally the northbound highway intersects these swampless barrens, but just above the highway, and behind the screen of dry scrub, every creeklet expands into a broad ribbon of swamp, a sure haven for grouse.

Here, come October, I sit in the solitude of my tamaracks and hear the hunters' cars roaring up the highway, hell-bent for the crowded counties to the north. I chuckle as I picture their dancing speedometers, their strained faces, their eager eyes glued on the northward horizon. At the noise of their passing, a cock grouse drums his defiance. My dog grins as we note his direction. That fellow, we agree, needs some exercise; we shall look him up presently.

The tamaracks grow not only in the swamp, but at the foot of the bordering upland, where springs break forth. Each spring has become choked with moss, which forms a boggy terrace. I call these terraces the hanging gardens, for out of their sodden muck the fringed gentians have lifted blue jewels. Such an October gentian, dusted with tamarack gold, is worth a full stop and a long look, even when the dog signals a grouse ahead.

Between each hanging garden and the creekside is a moss-paved deer trail, handy for the hunter to follow, and for the flushed grouse to cross – in a split second. The question is whether the bird and the gun agree on how a second should be split. If they do not, the next deer that passes finds a pair of empty shells to sniff at, but no feathers.

Higher up the creeklet I encounter an abandoned farm. I try to read, from the age of the young jackpines marching across an old field, how long ago the luckless farmer found out that sand plains were meant to grow solitude, not corn. Jackpines tell tall tales to the unwary, for they put on several whorls of branches each year, instead of only one. I find a better chronometer in an elm seedling that now blocks the barn doors. Its rings date back to the drought of 1930. Since that year no man has carried milk out of this barn.

I wonder what this family thought about when their mortgage finally outgrew their crops, and thus gave the signal for their eviction. Many thoughts, like flying grouse, leave no trace of their passing, but some leave clues that outlast the decades. He who, in some forgotten April, planted this lilac must have thought pleasantly of blooms for all the Aprils to come. She who used this washboard, its corrugations worn thin with many Mondays, may have wished for a cessation of all Mondays, and soon.

Musing on such questions, I become aware of the dog down by the spring, pointing patiently these many minutes. I walk up, apologizing for my inattention. Up twitters a woodcock, batlike, his salmon breast soaked in October sun. Thus goes the hunt.

It's hard on such a day to keep one's mind on grouse, for there are many distractions. I cross a buck track in the sand, and follow in idle curiosity. The track leads straight from one Jersey tea bush to another, with nipped twigs showing why.

This reminds me of my own lunch, but before I get it pulled out of my game pocket, I see a circling hawk, high skyward, needing identification. I wait till he banks and shows his red tail.

I reach again for the lunch, but my eye catches a peeled popple. Here a buck has rubbed off his itchy velvet. How long ago? The exposed wood is already brown; I conclude that horns must therefore be clean by now.

I reach again for the lunch, but am interrupted by an excited yawp from the dog, and a crash of bushes in the swamp. Out springs a buck, flag aloft, horns shining, his coat a sleek blue. Yes, the popple told the truth.

This time I get the lunch all the way out and sit down to eat. A chickadee watches me, and grows confidential about his lunch. He doesn't say what he ate, perhaps it was cool turgid ant-eggs, or some other avian equivalent of cold roast grouse.

Lunch over, I regard a phalanx of young tamaracks, their golden lances thrusting skyward. Under each the needles of yesterday fall to earth, building a blanket of smoky gold; at the tip of each the bud of tomorrow, preformed, poised, awaits another spring.

❖

One way to hunt partridge is to make a plan, based on logic and probabilities, of the terrain to be hunted. This will take you over the ground where the birds ought to be.

Another way is to wander, quite aimlessly, from one red lantern to another. This will likely take you where the birds actually are. The lanterns are blackberry leaves, red in October sun.

Red lanterns have lighted my way on many a pleasant hunt in many a region, but I think that blackberries must first have learned to glow in the sand counties of central Wisconsin. Along the little boggy streams of these friendly wastes, called poor by those whose own lights barely flicker, the blackberries burn richly red on every sunny day from first frost to the last day of the season. Every woodcock and every partridge has his private solarium under these briars. Most hunters, not knowing this, wear themselves out in the briarless scrub, and, returning home birdless, leave the rest of us in peace.

By 'us' I mean the birds, the stream, the dog, and myself. The stream is a lazy one; he winds through the alders as if he would rather stay here than reach the river. So would I. Every one of his hairpin hesitations means that much more streambank where hillside briars adjoin dank beds of frozen ferns and jewelweeds on the boggy bottom. No partridge can long absent himself from such a place, nor can I. Partridge hunting, then, is a creekside stroll, upwind, from one briar patch to another.

The dog, when he approaches the briars, looks around to make sure I am within gunshot. Reassured, he advances with stealthy caution, his wet nose screening a hundred scents for that one scent, the potential presence of which gives life and meaning to the whole landscape. He is the prospector of the air, perpetually searching its strata for olfactory gold. Partridge scent is the gold standard that relates his world to mine.

My dog, by the way, thinks I have much to learn about partridges, and, being a professional naturalist, I agree. He persists in tutoring me, with the calm patience of a professor of logic, in the art of drawing deductions from an educated nose. I delight in seeing him deduce a conclusion, in the form of a point, from data that are obvious to him, but speculative to my unaided eye. Perhaps he hopes his dull pupil will one day learn to smell.

Like other dull pupils, I know when the professor is right, even though I do not know why. I check my gun and walk in. Like any good professor, the dog never laughs when I miss, which is often. He gives me just one look, and proceeds up the stream in quest of another grouse.

Following one of these banks, one walks astride two landscapes, the hillside one hunts from, and the bottom the dog hunts in. There is a special charm in treading soft dry carpets of Lycopodium to flush birds out of the bog, and the first test of a partridge dog is his willingness to do the wet work while you parallel him on the dry bank.

A special problem arises where the belt of alders widens, and the dog disappears from view. Hurry at once to a knoll or point, where you stand stock-still, straining eye and ear to follow the dog. A sudden scattering of whitethroats may reveal his whereabouts. Again you may hear him breaking a twig, or splashing in a wet spot, or plopping into the creek. But when all sound ceases, be ready for instant action, for he is likely on point. Listen now for the premonitory clucks a frightened partridge gives just before flushing. Then follows the hurtling bird, or perhaps two of them, or I have known as many as six, clucking and flushing one by one, each sailing high for his own destination in the uplands. Whether one passes within gunshot is of course a matter of chance, and you can compute the chance if you have time: 360 degrees divided by 30, or whatever segment of the circle your gun covers. Divide again by 3 or 4, which is your chance of missing, and you have the probability of actual feathers in the hunting coat.

The second test of a good partridge dog is whether he reports for orders after such an episode. Sit down and talk it over with him while he pants. Then look for the next red lantern, and proceed with the hunt.

The October breeze brings my dog many scents other than grouse, each of which may lead to its own peculiar episode. When he points with a certain humorous expression of the ears, I know he has found a bedded rabbit. Once a dead-serious point yielded no bird, but still the dog stood frozen; in a tuft of sedge under his very nose was a fat sleeping coon, getting his share of October sun. At least once on each hunt the dog bays a skunk, usually in some

175

denser-than-ordinary thicket of blackberries. Once the dog pointed in midstream: a whir of wings upriver, followed by three musical cries, told me he had interrupted a wood duck's dinner. Not infrequently he finds jacksnipe in heavily pastured alders, and lastly he may put out a deer, bedded for the day on a high streambank flanked by alder bog. Has the deer a poetical weakness for singing waters, or a practical liking for a bed that cannot be approached without making a noise? Judging by the indignant flick of his great white flag it might be either, or both.

Almost anything may happen between one red lantern and another.

At sunset on the last day of the grouse season, every blackberry blows out his light. I do not understand how a mere bush can thus be infallibly informed about the Wisconsin statutes, nor have I ever gone back next day to find out. For the ensuing eleven months the lanterns glow only in recollection. I sometimes think that the other months were constituted mainly as a fitting interlude between Octobers, and I suspect that dogs, and perhaps grouse, share the same view.

— Sharon Anderson

Mel Ellis, whom The Milwaukee Journal *called a "poet of the land," was arguably Wisconsin's most popular outdoor writer. Before his death in 1984 at age 72, Ellis wrote hundreds or articles and short stories for national magazines. He also wrote 20 books, most notably* Wild Goose, Brother Goose, *and* Run, Rainey, Run, *chronicling the adventures of his German shorthair pointer.*

Ellis, born and raised Juneau, also was an associate editor of Field & Stream *for 12 years and was a syndicated columnist for the Associated Press. He wrote full time for* The Milwaukee Journal *from 1948 to 1963, and is best remembered for his column, "Notes From Little Lakes," which later appeared in* Wisconsin Sportsman *magazine from the early 1970s until Ellis' death. The column told of life on 15 acres near Big Bend in Waukesha County, where Ellis worked for decades converting pasture land into an arboretum with spring-fed ponds, thousands of trees, and fields of wildflowers.*

Ellis' writing centered around a deep love for the land. "Who has always, in manner mysterious, calmed my tortured spirit, strengthened my dwindling reserve, restored my faith and fostered such courage as brings me not only anxious but also exalting right into the face of an unpredictable tomorrow?" he once wrote. "It is the land, always the land! My womb and my tomb."

Pearl Diver
by
Mel Ellis

I am always going back to see if the big, black clams still cluster along the clay bottoms of the winding Rock River, hoping to find one with a pearl luminous as the moon. It is an unfinished piece of business which has been smoldering like gold fever since the day, as a sun-dried crisp of a boy, my questing thumb felt through a mess of clam meat and juice, touched the first hard nubbin of pearl, and turned it to the light where it flashed pale pink and white and light blue in the blazing sun. I held the seed pearl in the palm of my callused hand, and my fingers, with their ragged nails, trembled so much the pearl quivered with opalescent light. Then and there, any plans my mother had for making me into a concert violinist drained like rain off a hill to become one with my mysterious river.

The idea that my beautiful and bountiful river could hold such riches as might tempt grown men came late in life. I was already ten, and though I knew where the terns and coots nested, what sloughs to spear carp in, what bays held the largest northerns, which gravel bars the walleyes came to after dark, I had never dreamed that somewhere along that coppery river might rest a clam with a pearl big as a pigeon's egg and brilliant as the flame of the candle which each night lighted the way to my cot on the porch.

Subsequently I found many pearls. Never the perfect pearl, but rare beauties nevertheless – some pink, some white, and a few as black and shiny as a drip of tar. But in the miraculous instant that I brought that first tiny pearl out of obscurity, I was caught up and consumed by the promise of such riches as all prospectors must dream about. I became feverish with such anticipation that the catching of ten-pound fish was relegated to the realm of triviality. Looking back now, I can well understand and appreciate the visions that must have compelled prospectors to die crossing the desert and mountain in quest of treasure.

Fifty years ago, clamming along the Mississippi and other midwestern rivers was still a thriving business because synthetics hadn't yet replaced the pearl button. Itinerant wraiths of women in gingham and overalled men roamed hopefully and unobtrusively from river to river, searching for the big one, but settling mainly for seed pearls which were sold for ornamenting other jewelry. They earned just about enough to keep them in bread and whiskey. And though they never quite reached it, they were trying for the rainbow.

In the beginning, I knew nothing of pearls, nothing of the men who hunted them. Then one night, having gone to my cot, I lay listening for the splash of fish on the river, the inquiry of a night heron looking to camp, the whimper of the little owls in the oaks. I heard them all, and also a mallard quacking in alarm. Then came a strange sound, and lifting to an elbow so I could look through the screen, I saw flashlight beams crisscrossing the glade.

Next morning there was a tent, and I discovered that one woman and two men had moved in during the night, though for what – since they had no fish poles – I couldn't imagine. When they began bringing boatloads of big, black clams to shore, when they sat cross-legged opening them, discarding the shell and flesh, I was mystified. But having, like a young brush buck, an aversion to coming too close to strangers, I stayed my distance and waited until that night to ask my father what they might be doing.

"Likely looking for pearls," he said.

Pearls! In my Rock River! Right here in the black clams which were so plentiful that walking over a bed of them was like walking across a field of stones.

I didn't sleep much that night. The next morning I threaded my duck skiff along their trail, careful to stay a respectable distance, and when they began collecting clams I put out some cane poles – with no bait on the hooks – so they wouldn't know I was spying. The men, without removing any of their clothes, waded chest deep in the river, feeling for the clams with their feet and dunking at intervals to bring them up. When they had a boat loaded, they rowed to the nearest shore and began to open them and search for pearls.

I wrapped and stowed my poles and hastened around a bend so I'd be out of sight. Then I began collecting clams. When I had a black mound of them in the stern of the little skiff, I paddled back to the cottage, got a knife, and sat down to open them. But it wasn't that easy. The harder I tried, the tighter the clams closed their shells. I tried smashing them between two rocks. They broke open, but the flesh was crushed and juice spattered on my bare legs. I scraped and bruised and cut my fingers, but I found no pearls.

It had been obvious that the men had no difficulty in opening the clams, so I bided my time, and when they were once again hunched over a mound of black shells, I crept through the grass to where I could watch. It was instantly clear that the knives they were using were thrust to a point just above the hinge and then rocked back and forth. I backed carefully away and then went back to my own pile of clams. I made a few false passes with the knife, but when I hit the muscle, the clam relaxed and I could pry the shells apart. Then I went carefully through the meat, and though I found a few pearls, they were encrusted in the shell and irretrievable.

I remember as though it were yesterday when I finished with the last clam. The sun was boiling down out of a brassy sky. A cloud of flies had descended on the clams and me. My fingers were criss-crossed with cuts. The clam juice was congealing on my body in uncomfortable and alien scabs. In the end, it was the flies rather than an overwhelming desire to find pearls which drove me back into the river to get another load of clams.

I went through the whole painful procedure again, but found no pearls. I think that might have ended it, but the next day when I walked into Juneau to deliver bullheads to the Northwestern Hotel, the bartender showed me three seed pearls which he had taken in payment for some moonshine. I knew at once they had come from the professional pearlers camped beneath my porch.

He let me hold the pearls, and though they were neither large nor perfectly round, they were beautiful. One was snow-white, another was pink as a sunset, and the third was black and shiny as a speck of coal. I completed my bullhead deliveries on the run so I could get back to my skiff for another try at pearling.

I don't remember exactly, but I think I went for three days without finding a pearl. Then one day when the men were out on the river, I found enough courage to approach the woman who stayed in the camp and did the cooking. She looked terribly old, though I don't suppose she was more than forty. She was fat and wore a man's shoes without any socks inside, and though I didn't get close, I could smell moonshine. Her hair came down from a bun on her head in ragged strands like horsehair from an oriole nest which has been in the wind so long it has started unraveling. She was sitting on a stump drinking coffee from a tin cup when I came up, and for a while she just looked at me. I was about to turn and run when she said, "Yes, Boy?"

It was a strangely wonderful voice, deep and throaty. It stopped me in my tracks. Although she had spoken but two words, it came to me at once that she was lonely and beaten and sad. I stared a long time before I realized I was staring. Then, to cover up, I said, "Could I ask you some questions?"

She laughed a little, and the sound of her laughter was as soothing as the sound of her voice. She replied, "Well, I guess so, because I don't have to answer them if I don't want to."

I looked down at my feet. I don't suppose I looked up at her once while I was talking. Perhaps sensing that I was frightened, she told me to sit down, and asked if I'd like some coffee. I took the coffee. It was so bitter I could hardly swallow it, but I made a pretense of drinking. After a while she asked, "What do you want to know?"

So, still looking at my feet, I explained that I wanted to learn how to find pearls, that I knew about getting the shells open, but that I didn't know how to go through the clam meat without dumping it into a pail and fingering through it.

She got up and went to a pile of empty clamshells. A cyclone of flies lifted as she bent over to get one. Then she came back to the stump and told me to watch while she ran her thumbs along each side of the shell under the meat to the spots where the pearls – if there were any – usually lay. In a low, hoarse voice that was almost a whisper, she explained that you had to feel the pearls rather than see them, and that it was even good to shut your eyes while thumbing along beneath the meat so as to be able to concentrate on the sense of touch.

"When you feel one you'll know it," she said. "Then get it between your thumb and forefinger and put it up under your upper lip where it'll be safe. Then when you've sucked it clean, spit it into a small bottle."

Then she was silent. After a time, I dared to look into her face and ask, "Is that all there's to it?"

She gave her tin cup a toss and coffee grounds went spraying into a clump of cattails. She looked into the bottom of the cup as though there might be a pearl in it, and then she said, "That's all. That's all that you'd understand." She got up heavily and sighed.

"Thank you," I said, turning away.

Out of the corner of my eye I saw her turn toward me again, so I waited. She put a hand to her face and then said quietly, "Don't thank me, Boy. It's no life, believe me. Forget the pearls. You'll starve trying."

I doubt that I understood at the time what she was trying to say to me, but I waited until she went into the tent. Then I walked as far as it was necessary for politeness before breaking into a gallop.

It wasn't until the next day that I felt the first nubbin beneath my thumb and brought the first seed pearl to the light of day. It was almost as big as a perch's eye, and though not completely round, it had such color as took my breath away. I quickly put it into my mouth, sucked it clean, and then, holding a small medicine bottle to my lips, spit the pearl into it. It shone like captured sunshine, and I just had to sit and marvel at it though every fiber of my being was for getting on with my search for greater riches. I found two smaller ones that day. Even my family was excited by my discovery. We sat around the kerosene lamp until way past my bedtime admiring and talking about the pearls.

After that, there was no time for anything else. My bullhead customers began to complain; Buck, my dog, had a droopy, sad look in his eye because I had no time to hunt and swim with him; my brothers and sisters took to whispering about me; and the fishermen who saw me armpit deep on a bed, feeling for clams with my feet, asked what the crazy kid was up to. I grew lean as a heron. My skin got a leathery look. There were circles under my eyes because I got up so early and was still opening clams long after the mosquitoes had claimed the night as their own.

But when I got back into shoes to go to school, I had a small wine glass full of some of the most beautiful pearls a man could ever want to see. I used to spread them on a card table and sit by the hour while the light, like the notes of a song, played a hundred variations on the same theme. None of the pearls was round enough to be worth much money. I knew that, but it made no difference because I didn't want to sell them anyway. When my father suggested I take them to the jeweler to see how much I could get for them, I always found some excuse for putting it off.

Then came the day when I went next door to show the pearls to my grandmother's new boarder. I had spread them on the card table, when Buck came running through the room and upset the table. All the pearls went down the large, circular, hot-air register of my grandmother's furnace.

I nearly died. And sometimes I think a tiny part of me did. I braved the searing heat and went through the dust and grime which had been accumulating in the old furnace for years, but I never found one of my precious pearls. I figured I had wasted my entire summer, but now that I look back, I know that the summer wasn't wasted.

Now I know that the real value was not in the pearls but in the dream. I have never dreamed so grandly since, and in all the years between, I have never come to any adventure with such a singleness of purpose. And in losing the pearls, I learned the hardest lesson: All life is transient. Only the dreams endure.

– Sharon Anderson

Dan Small, of Belgium, is a full-time freelance writer and television producer. Since its premier in 1984, he has been the host and producer of "Outdoor Wisconsin," a weekly television show seen on public television in 12 states.

Small, who holds a Ph.D. in French literature from Rice University, serves as Outdoor Writer in Residence at Northland College in Ashland. He is a past recipient (1990) of the Gordon MacQuarrie Award for excellence in environmental communication, from the Wisconsin Academy of Sciences, Arts and Letters; in 1986 he was named Conservation Communicator of the Year by the Wisconsin Wildlife Federation.

Small is the author of Fish Wisconsin *and co-author of* The Official Outdoor Wisconsin Cookbook. *He is a field editor for* Wisconsin Outdoor Journal *and a regular contributor to* Wisconsin Sportsman *and* Petersen's Hunting. *His articles have appeared in many other regional and national magazines.*

He has hunted and fished in literally every corner of Wisconsin, but Small's favorite haunts are the Bayfield County shores and tributaries of Gitchee Gumee.

Steelhead Dues
by
Dan Small

Found another dead bird under the picture window by the feeder this morning. Its almost weightless body was still warm when I held it. Three tiny feathers clung to a moist spot on the pane, which in this light reflects an inviting sky and hedgerow. How many do we kill this way compared to the number that survive the winter because we feed them so well?

A thrush this time, not a pedestrian sparrow or chickadee, but which one? Olive back, rusty rump patch, faint eye ring – my field guide tells me it's a Swainson's, with a rising flute-like call that will not echo in the woods this spring. Last victim was a purple finch, a sunflower seed still tight in its bill . . .

A stubborn patch of old snow lingers under the big spruce east of the barn, and a ridge of the stuff along the porch reminds me of the hours spent pushing it off the roof after every winter storm. The bare expanse of yard is still too dormant to call a lawn and too sodden to rake; driveway's too muddy to think about taking off the snow tires just yet. Ragged end of a northern April.

Early steelheaders in their four-wheel-drives have deeply rutted the old river road, but the clay track is firm now and it is no problem to avoid the deeper holes. There are no other cars at the dead-end turnaround – it looks as though I may have this stretch of river to myself.

Pulling on my waders, I strain to push one foot home, then the other, and hope the extra pair of socks I'm wearing will keep the chill off long enough to let me spend a couple hours knee-deep in ice water. I snug my rod sections together with a quarter-twist and slam the trunk shut, then step off the road toward the river.

Generations of booted feet have etched a path deep into the heavy red clay soil, the same soil that transforms the normally placid river into a torrent the color of tomato soup after every spring downpour.

As I slog through the bottoms near the river, the squealing departure of a pair of wood ducks from a snowmelt pool takes me back to fall hunts in this same flooded timber. They circle once for a look at what spooked them, then bank and climb over the trees as I step into the waiting river.

The river carries just enough runoff color today to darken it a shade and obscure the deeper sections, but I can see my boot a foot or so beneath the surface. Tiny ridges on every sandbar, like miniature canyon shelves, tell me the water has dropped steadily this past week. I have picked my morning with luck. Spring conditions on this river are rarely as good as this.

Two generations ago, lumberjacks cleared the entire watershed of pines – and there were plenty – baring the river's sand and clay banks to the savage bite of spring runoff. Storms have leveled its bed for a mile at a stretch. Today, cattle graze right to its banks and gas pipelines cross it in several places. The river's scoured pools hold few resident trout anymore, but Lake Superior's steelhead still run to its spring-fed headwaters every April to spawn, and a handful of resolute anglers try their best to intercept them.

As I stand in the shallows stringing my rod, the drake wood duck returns with a rip and plops into a backwater just downstream. I have barely time to look up before he realizes his mistake and blasts off again. There are no nest boxes along the river here; this pair must have found a suitable woodpecker hole in a snag nearby.

Fingers still warm enough to respond quickly snell a hook to the end of my line and dig through my vest for a package of green yarn. Like most steelheaders, I have slowly progressed from spawn sacks to yarn. There is nothing so inglorious as a gob of fish eggs balled up in nylon mesh, so you eventually add a tag of bright yarn to your egg baits to dress them up a bit and give them respectability.

Sooner or later, you take the purist plunge and forego the spawn altogether, perhaps in the self-deception that you are "fly fishing" – for most call the half-inch "wings" of yarn they tuck into a hand-tied snell "yarn flies." Yarn manufacturers know better. They have given their dyed synthetics names far more mundane than those bestowed upon the delicate lures of the dry-fly purist. No Quill Gordons or Light Cahills here, but such hues as "flame," "nugget," "egg," "moss," "apricot," "cerise," "chartreuse" and "baby pink."

Still, yarn has advantages over spawn. It stays supple, has no odor to lose and its color won't wash out. Unless you break it off on a snag or tire of using the same color, one yarn fly will last all day. Spawn quickly fades, hardens and loses its taste in cold water – especially if it has been stored frozen. Yarn is also cheaper to buy and easier to tie up. But yarn's real edge is simpler still – it catches fewer suckers and more steelhead.

For some reason, Superior's steelhead prefer the green shades over the more natural colors. Today I opt for chartreuse over moss because the slightly turbid river calls for a little brighter bait. I snip off a small piece, snug it to the hook and begin working my way upstream, slowly probing each hole, each run.

We are three weeks into the season and others have been hitting the streams in earnest with only moderate success. This is my first time out. On warmer mornings, the smell of spawn often hangs like a promise over the river, thick with fish fresh from the lake. Today, there is only the faint odor of skunk cabbage, and the smoky waters do not reveal their secret. The fish should be up, but I will have to work to find out.

Whup . . . *Whup* . . . *Whup* . . . I always mistake those first few thumps for my own heartbeat gone wild, but then the pulse quickens and I know somewhere up ahead a grouse is drumming. As I round each bend, his muted roll seems to float on upriver, coming first from one bank, then the other. Near a deep, narrow channel where the river once bent sharply south, I finally come abreast of him. He must be a hundred yards or so back in the cedars on the north bank, blindly banging out his act of faith that there are lady grouse within earshot.

Every spring after ice-out, this river holds a surprise or two, for it changes its course more than any other I have known. For years, a massive log jam shored up a narrow bank just here in a hairpin bend. A spring flood finally washed out both the jam and the bank a couple years ago, and now the old channel is dry. I walk the hairpin and peek up under exposed roots and undercuts that provided wayside shelter for migrant trout, but which now gape at an empty streambed and wait for time and succession to cover them as the river once did.

The channel's upstream end is completely silted in and sedges have sodded it over. In a few years the alders will have found sure footing in the former streambed, and no newcomer to the river will ever guess it was once two bends and a hundred yards longer here.

An hour of bumping yarn along the bottom in every likely gravel run and hole has produced not a single strike, but the chill has drained the feeling from my hands, so I concentrate harder on trying to read the Braille signals my rod is sending. Every spring my fingers must learn to read this language anew, and I can't help but wonder how many discriminating steelhead have gently tasted and rejected my fluffy offering before the first heedless fish nailed it like the delight he has sought all his life.

The next hole runs deep from bank to bank. I sacrifice the near side and stretch out to fish the other, letting my yarn drift tight against the far shore. But after ten minutes of playing London Bridge, both shoulders ache and I lower the rod to give them a rest. Just then I feel a touch and sweep the rod skyward . . . too late! I have a fish on for two tugs, then my hook sails harmlessly over my head.

Now I comb the hole with new intensity. A minute later a pass draws another strike. My spirits jump as I set the hook and it holds, but the fish turns easily after its first run. A sucker. The next drift yields another sucker, so I move on, doubtful now about the fish I lost earlier, but warmed a little nonetheless by the pull of those two suckers in fast current.

Around the next bend I work up through a slower, deeper run below a shallow riffle. Fishless, I am about to move on when a fish surfaces near a boulder at the tail of the run. I ease back downstream, and on the third pass near the rock where I saw it splash, the fish takes.

A steelhead this time! I tighten up and the bright fish shatters the surface and tailwalks the length of the run before throwing the hook. Shaken, I sit on a boulder for a minute or two to let this new fact sink in. There is at least one steelhead in the river, and I have had him on momentarily.

I wait five minutes and try near the rock again. Another fish takes and this time the hookup is solid. This steelhead jumps twice, then runs to the head of the pool and leaps again. Like most lake-run rainbows, this fish fights as if possessed. All I can do is hold the rod high while it runs and attempt to bow to its leaps. It spends itself quickly, but comes to net with the devil still in its eyes.

It is a hen, fresh from the lake and still plump with spawn, a faint pink stripe beginning to show through the silver of its sides. Cradling this cool, taut life in my hands I remember the thrush's warm but slack body I held a few hours ago. I support the fish gently in the current till its strength returns, then it shudders and spurts from my hands.

By now, the sun has warmed the river some, and an occasional fish flashes as it struggles to hold in a swift run. My legs do not feel the slight rise in water temperature, for they have gone quite numb. But my wool jacket holds the sun's welcome warmth over my stiff shoulders.

Two holes further above I am into my third steelhead, another fresh fish that would rather jump than swim. This one heads downstream on its first run and I stumble and splash along behind it, rod held high to keep my line from looping around a boulder. I manage to turn the fish just short of a shallow rapids and get him heading upstream. A premature pass with the net sends him leaping away again, but after one more run he quits suddenly and comes in on his side.

This one is a sleek male, about six pounds. His stripe is more vivid than the hen's and his back is just beginning to darken. As I lift him from the net, leaking milt betrays his condition. I break his neck with a snap and hold his quivering body till it becomes still. It has been months since I have eaten a fresh trout. I dress him quickly, rinsing his coral flesh in an eddy, and watch his blood merge with the river's current.

I climb the steep ridge path, one numbed finger hooked in the throat of my dripping prize. At the top of the slope I pause to catch my breath near the remains of an old cabin. Ten years ago its roof and walls held out the weather, but vandals, porcupines and decay have taken their toll. Part of one wall still stands, its lone window frame clinging stubbornly to a few jagged shards of pane, but the others have toppled into the ravine, and the roof now lies on the rotted floorboards.

Each time I pass here, I wonder what dreams he sought to fulfill, the man who built this cabin overlooking the river. No doubt he, too, took an occasional April steelhead for his evening meal. What a wildlife parade he must have enjoyed from this window that now stares vacantly across the clearing that was his modest front yard. Did he ever find beneath it on an April morning, the slack body of a thrush that mistook its blue reflection for the sky?

❧

– Sharon Anderson

Frances Hamerstrom, former debutante and fashion model, is best known as a naturalist and a writer. She and her late husband, Frederick, were students of Aldo Leopold. The husband and wife biologist team were responsible for establishing a part of the Buena Vista marsh as a refuge for one of Wisconsin's remnant populations of prairie chicken, a species they studied extensively.

Hamerstrom, who lives near Plainfield, has written more than 100 scientific papers, articles and reviews, as well as ten cookbooks, including the Wild Food Cookbook, and two children's books. She has lectured in more than a dozen countries and in 1993 was recipient of the Gordon MacQuarrie Award.

Also, she has hunted every season since 1920. The accompanying story is taken from her book Is She Coming Too?, which chronicles her hunting adventures as well as barriers she had to overcome in pursuing a sport that was traditionally the province of men.

Drifting Down The Yellow
by
Frances Hamerstrom

Frederick hates portages. I'm more of a romantic type and am willing to put up with quite a lot of inconvenience to hunt wood ducks along a river that seems so wild and untravelled as to be almost pristine. Year after year I have allowed myself one day to float down the Yellow River. Year after year I invite Frederick to join me. His refusal to join this worthy hunt is always courteous and always firm. So I go alone.

My preparations start the day before. I load the duck boat on top of the station wagon, put my bicycle, gun, shells, paddles, and lunch inside. I take along an axe and plenty of matches.

It's still dark when I start out and very, very cold. My only worry is that the wood ducks may have pulled out – not that some of the ice may be too thick for river travel. Day is just breaking when I get to Necedah and hide my bicycle in a jackpine thicket near the river.

194

I drive the eleven road miles upstream to Sprague as quickly as possible, pull the boat off the top of the car, and load my gear into it. I close the car windows as it might snow.

The current is pretty swift and soon I'm paddling downstream at a great clip. I sing to myself "Paddling down the Yellow – just to shoot some ducks." When I get close to the first big oaks near the bank I stop singing and drift with my gun on the ready. Woodies might be gobbling acorns right within range.

The coves are iced up but the main channel is fast moving. A fallen maple bars my way. It's a two minute job to clear a path with the axe – or at least ten minutes to unload, pull the boat around on shore and load up again.

The axe is not where I thought I'd put it. It's still back in the car!

By noon I had lost track of my portages. Only one was memorable. I was just unloading the boat for another long pull through the vegetation when one lone wood duck whizzed upstream. I dropped it neatly on some ice, and, as neatly, went over the tops of my hip boots on the retrieve.

So I pulled off my boots, wrung the water out of my socks and decided to travel barefoot for a while – that is, until the next portage. Even my tough feet are tenderer when cold, and my toes are digging in to pull a rather heavy boat. I put my wet boots back on and ate lunch. The banana I'd brought along for dessert was not exactly frozen – just black and frost-filled.

It was quiet – wondrously quiet except for chickadees near my lunch spot and the sudden slap of a beaver's tail – close, nearby and upstream – and I'd never noticed the cuttings! The wood duck in the bow of the boat gave me great pleasure.

Frederick and I tend to study a map and plan each hunt, but this was different – it was my private hunt. I didn't have a map with me and, nothing, not even a bottle, can get lost drifting down a river. Pretty soon the river would widen and this would mean the end of portages. The uneasy feeling that there had been more blowdowns and more portages made me suspect I was behind even my nebulous schedule.

Just as the river finally widened I jumped a duck which tried to fly and then just skittered on ice away into a cove – a cripple. I suppose it took me a good half hour to break the ice with a paddle and get close enough to finish off that duck – a skinny one at that.

Now to paddle for all I was worth to get downstream to my bicycle. Ice – thicker and thicker ice, barred my way. I tried walking the shore and pulling the boat on top of the ice. And then I'd try wading and pushing it. Sometimes I'd find stretches of open water and paddle, but there weren't many such "vacations."

Twilight merged into deep dusk and the blackness of night. I hugged the west bank of the river, plodding, pushing, busting ice. Frederick and the children were undoubtedly eating supper by the big wood stove, but I just wanted to see the light of some farmhouse – and then I did, a light! It was way across on the far side of the river. Without hesitation I broke a trail through the ice toward that light.

Farmers are said to go to bed early so – with plenty of noise – I whacked my way toward the farm and beached the boat. The light was still in sight, but not very close. I pushed through some bushes and found a trail – actually a sort of fishing trail that led to the house. I banged on the back door.

"May I leave my boat by the river for a while?"

The farmer gasped. "You come by boat?" he sputtered.

"Come in, come in and get warm."

"Here, Mother, give the lady a cup of coffee."

"No, I've got to get to my bicycle – thank you so much. It's all right to leave the boat isn't it?"

"Yes, but . . . "

"I'll hitchhike."

I started down that sandy road, hoping for a ride. And then, remembering that state law forbade anyone to get into a car with an uncased gun, I quickly hid my Parker and marked the spot well – by a fence.

No cars passed, but the ducks seemed to get heavy. So I hung my precious ducks on a maple and marked the spot with a foot drag across the sandy road. Then I went on south – after about a mile I slowed up and took stock:

1. My boat is at that farm
2. My gun is hidden by that fence
3. My ducks are hanging in that maple
4. My bicycle is in that thicket near Necedah
5. My car is near Sprague

And Furthermore . . .

6. It is night
7. It is cold
8. My boots are heavy
9. There is no traffic

I plodded on just thinking about little things like getting blisters on my heels. When a car finally came I stood in the middle of that sand road with my arms outspread and brought it to a full stop. The man who drove it was full of questions.

"You live near here?"

"No."

"You got folks in Necedah?"

"No."

"What you wanna go to Necedah for?"

"I have a bicycle in Necedah."

The moon came out. It was warm in the car. I dozed off.

"Where is your bicycle at?"

"Just north of town in a pine thicket."

"I'll take you there."

He sounded more disbelieving than gallant and when he stopped, he didn't say good-bye. He just watched to see if I was really going to come out of that thicket with a bicycle. I did. And I waved. He shook his head and drove away.

It was eleven long miles to the car. Farms were about half a mile apart along the river road. Each farm had at least one dog, some had many more. It soon became plain to me that all these dogs had spent their lives waiting for the Great Moment – namely on a glorious moonlight night, one female would try to pedal past them while they growled, barked, and grabbed at her legs with their teeth.

When I reached the car, it was a great temptation to close the doors firmly (against prowling dogs) and sleep – just for a little while in the back of the station wagon. But Frederick would worry.

I put the bicycle in the back of the station wagon instead, and drove back past all those dogs, delightfully secure with the doors closed and the windows rolled up. I found my sand scruff, climbed up into the maple and took my ducks down; I found the fence and picked up my Parker, then I found the farm and drove down to the river to load my boat onto the car. Two dogs showed less than a helpful spirit, but lights went on in the farmhouse and both dogs were called off.

It was only fifty miles back to our house. When I finally slid into bed next to Frederick I had been gone for about twenty hours.

"You had me worried," he said, and then asked, "Did you misjudge the distance?"

I had blisters on my heels, bruises from dog's teeth on my legs, and two wood ducks in the pump room.

I kept my answer simple.

"Yes."

❧

— Sandy Klein Stevens

More than 35 years after his death in 1956, Gordon MacQuarrie remains one of Wisconsin's best-loved outdoor writers. He is perhaps remembered most fondly for his Old Duck Hunters Association, Inc. stories, featuring Hizzoner, Mr. President (actually MacQuarrie's father-in-law) and himself. The stories appeared from the 1930s to 1950s in national outdoor periodicals and in The Milwaukee Journal, where "Mac" was outdoor editor from 1936 until the time of his death.

MacQuarrie, born in Superior in 1900, was a newspaper and magazine writer all of his life. After graduating from the University of Wisconsin with a degree in journalism in 1923 he went to work as a reporter for his hometown paper, The Superior Evening Telegram. He worked his way through the ranks of reporter and city editor at that newspaper before being promoted to managing editor in 1927. In 1936 he left Superior to become outdoor editor of The Milwaukee Journal.

Most of the Old Duck Hunters Association, Inc., stories are set in MacQuarrie's beloved northwest Wisconsin. The chronicles of the ODHA were posthumously published in book form as Stories of the Old Duck Hunters and Other Drivel, More Stories of the Old Duck Hunters, and Last Stories of the Old Duck Hunters. A fourth book, MacQuarrie Miscellany, contains not only ODHA stories but samples of other writings MacQuarrie did on the outdoors.

Today, Wisconsin's highest outdoor writer's recognition, The Gordon MacQuarrie Award, presented annually by the Wisconsin Academy of Sciences, Arts and Letters, is named in his honor.

In The Presence of
Mine Enemies

by
Gordon MacQuarrie

The dusk of late duck season was hurrying westward across the sky and slanting snow was whitening the street gutters as I turned into the automotive emporium of the President of the Old Duck Hunters' Association, Inc. The man in the parts department explained that Hizzoner was out on the used-car lot. There I found him, thoughtfully kicking a tire on an august and monstrous second-hand car, soon to be taking the Association on its final expedition of the season.

"We could try Libby Bay again," he reflected. "But the Hole in the Wall will be frozen. Jens says every bluebill on Dig Devil's has hauled his freight. Shallow Bay'd be open at the narrows, but I s'pose Joe's hauled in all his boats. Phoned Hank. He said there's an inch of ice on Mud Lake and she's making fast."

He went over other possibilities. The situation was urgent, for only a few days remained of the season. The widespread below the Copper Dam of the St. Croix? "Might not see a thing 'cept sawbills." The grassy island in the open water of the St. Louis River? "Too much big water to buck in this wind." Taylor's Point on the Big Eau Claire? "Wind's wrong for it and she's gonna stay in that quarter."

Street lights came on and home-going city toilers bent into the growing storm with collars turned up. One of them crossed the street and tried the showroom door which the parts man had just locked. Mister President called from the lot, "Something I can do for you?"

"Ye're dern tootin!" came the reply. "Open up this dump and let a man get warm."

Mister President grinned. "It's Chad," he said, making haste to unlock the showroom door.

Anyone in that community on reasonable terms with the way of the duck, the trout, the partridge and the white-tailed deer knows Chad just as he knows Mister President. Before the days when I cut myself in as an apprentice, the ODHA had consisted almost solely of Mister President and Chad. In recent years they get together only a couple of times per year on outdoor missions which can be anything from looking up old trout holes to picking blueberries.

But they meet regularly in church, except during the duck season and possibly two or three Sundays in late May or early June when the shadflies hatch. Chad is an especially stout pillar of the church, and passes the collection plate with a stern and challenging eye on the brethren he considers too thrifty.

The belligerent affection which Hizzoner and Chad reciprocate was once amply demonstrated at a Men's Club meeting in the church basement when suggestions were called for.

"Get a one-armed guy to take Chad's job passing the plate," volunteered Mister President.

Chad, who came upon holiness late in life and became so enchanted with Biblical wisdom that he quotes verses every chance, snorted back, "Let him who is without sin cast the first stone. . ."

"The time," Chad announced, "is short."

"There'll be no 14-year-old touring car with California top repaired here this night," declared Mister President. "Tell you what, though – bring it down to the lot and I'll give you $7.50 for it on a new job."

"My son, attend unto my wisdom," said Chad sagely. "Last deer season I was on a drive in back of Little Bass Lake. Found a spring-hole at the edge of a big marsh." His eyes gleamed with what is recognized in church as religious fervor. "No map shows it. Everything else in the country was froze up, and this little spring hole was open. There's a point of high, dry land poking into it. There's smartweed in there and watercress, and the day I saw it mallards jumped out of it."

"How about the road in?"

"We'll have to walk a mile."

Mister President frowned briefly, but Chad's mustache became a reasonable straight line as he intoned, "If thou faint in the day of adversity, thy strength is small."

"Let's at it, then," decided Mister President.

Quick getaways are no problem for the ODHA in the critical times of the season. At such times decoys are always sorted and sacked, shellboxes full and thermos bottles yawning for their soup and coffee. Against emergency conditions, Mister President also sets the old horse blanket and barn lantern conveniently at hand in the garage, for it is by these implements that he keeps warm in late-season blinds.

A mere accessory to their reunion, I drove the big car while the two cronies smoked and remembered. They agreed I'd come in handy toting gear and that I could be put to use if ice had to be broken. Objections on my part were swept away as Chad patted me on the back and said piously, "The righteous shall flourish like the palm tree."

Fine slanting snow darted across the path of the headlights. With that northwest wind I knew it would not snow much; but should the wind veer to the northeast, then we would be very happy at having the heavy, high-wheeled monster of a car for bucking drifts. It was a little after 9 P.M. when we disembarked beneath the high oaks which spread over Norm's place on the north shore of Big Yellow Lake, Burnett County, Wisconsin. Norm appeared with a flashlight.

"Might have known it'd be no one but you out on a night like this."

He lit an air-tight stove in an overnight cabin. Chad, police suspenders drooping as he readied for bed, set his old alarm clock with the bell on top for 5 A.M. A few minutes were allowed for final smokes and for further recollection of past delights. Chad had started to recall "the night we slept on the depot floor at Winnebojou" when a car entered the yard.

Again Norm emerged, prepared a cabin, and went back to sleep. As is always the way in duck camps, the newcomers pounded on our door for a pre-dawn investigation. As the two men entered, somewhat suspiciously I thought, Chad's face fell for a brief instant, but he made a quick recovery and fell upon the two hunters with vast friendship.

Where were they going to hunt in the morning? Weren't we all crazy for being out in such weather? How's the missus and the children?

Chad volunteered with bare-faced frankness that we were "going down the Yellow River a piece to that widespread just this side of Eastman's." Our visitors alleged they had it in mind to try the deep point in the cane grass across Big Yellow. Mister President and Chad solemnly agreed that sounded like a promising spot – "mighty promising."

The two departed for bed, and Chad cried after them cheerfully, "See you in church, boys!" The moment they were gone, Chad seized his alarm clock and set it to ring an hour earlier. "Those fakers aren't fooling me," he snorted.

"Me, either," said Mister President. "Somebody knows something."

"They were with me on that deer drive last fall. Gentlemen, say your prayers well tonight. There's only one spot on that marsh that's really any good, and that's the little spring-hole." He rolled in with a final muttering: "Deliver me from the workers of iniquity."

Within a few minutes the cabin resounded with the devout snores of Mister President and Chad. I lay awake a bit longer, listening to the wind in the oaks, weighing our chances for the morrow and marveling at the hypocritical poise of my comrades in the face of emergency. I knew those two adversaries of ours better than well. One was a piano tuner who, by some transference of vocational talent, could play a tune on a Model '97 that was strictly lethal so far as ducks are concerned. The other was a butcher likewise noted for his wing-shooting and his stoutness in going anywhere after ducks.

Mister President and Chad snored. The snow tapped on the window like fine sand, and then suddenly someone was shaking me m the dark. It was Mister President.

"Get up quietly," he hissed. "We beat the alarm clock so they wouldn't hear it. Don't turn on the light. Don't even strike a match!"

Like burglars we groped in the dark getting dressed and gathering up gear. "How about breakfast?" I asked. Mister President snickered, and Chad's voice came as from a sepulcher in the pitch dark: "Trust in the Lord and do good."

Softly we closed the door behind us and climbed into the car. Mister President got behind the wheel with Chad beside him and me alone in the back seat. The motor roared, headlights blazed and almost simultaneously a light went on in the cabin of our neighbors.

"Step on 'er!" Chad shouted, and the old crate made the snow fly as it leaped out of Norm's yard.

"We've got the jump on 'em," Chad exulted, but did not forget to add: "The righteous shall inherit the land and dwell forever."

It was a wild ride on a wild morning. The snow had stopped when two to three inches lay on the level. That was enough to make for skidding turns on the sharp corners where Mister President kept to maximum speed. We roared up steep hills and kept the power on going down. We passed white barns, ghostly and cold-looking in the dark, and at a field fronting a farmstead owned by one honorary member of the ODHA, Gus Blomberg, Chad ordered the car halted. He got out, took something from Gus's front yard that rattled like tin and stuffed it into the car trunk.

"What was it, Chad?" I asked.

"Out of the mouths of babes and fools," he retaliated, poked Mister President in the ribs and roared: "Step on 'er some more!" He shall deliver thee from the snare of the fowler!"

I knew part of the road. But after they skirted the base of the long point jutting into Little Bass Lake and took to pulp trails through the jack-pine barrens I was lost. Chad ordered "right," or 'left," or sometimes, "Don't forget to turn out for the big scrub-oak."

We labored up a hilltop on a barely discernible pair of ruts, and the big car came to a stop, practically buried in low scrub-oak. Instantly the lights were switched off, and Mister President and Chad listened for the sound of the enemy's motor. They heard nothing, but nevertheless hurried with the job of loading up with the sinews of war and heading for the spring-hole.

Only you who have been there know how a 60-pound sack of decoys in a Duluth pack-sack can cut into the shoulders when hands are occupied with gun and shellbox. Chad led the way in the dark and took us miraculously through the better parts of that oak and pine tangle. A half mile along the way we stopped to listen again, and this time we heard the motor of another car laboring up the hill through the scrub.

"Step on 'er again," counseled Chad, shouldering his burdens. "They haven't forgotten the way in, and that piano tuner can run like a deer!"

Chad permitted the use of lights now. We stumbled for what seemed miles until he led us down a gentle slope, and there before us was black, open water, about an acre of it. The omens were good. Mallards took off as a flashlight slit across the water.

"Keep the dang lights on all you want," said Mister President. "Let 'em know we're here fustest with the mostest."

Mister President and I spread his ancient decoys while Chad busied himself on a mysterious errand some distance away. As I uncoiled decoy strings I saw that the hole was a mere open dot in what must have been a large, flat marsh. Tall flaggers hemmed in the open water and stretched far beyond the range of the flashlight.

Mister President and I dug a pit in soft sand on fairly high ground and embroidered the edges of it with jack-pine and scrub-oak. We heard the piano tuner and the butcher push through the cover on the hill at our back, heard them panting and talking in low voices. Chad returned and boomed for all to hear: "Aint's a thing open but this one little patch. Betcha we don't see a feather here today!"

He fooled no one. The piano tuner and the butcher made a wide circle around us. We could hear them crashing through brush and Chad grudgingly allowed, "That butcher can hit the bush like a bull moose." Then we heard them walking across the marsh ice among the raspy flaggers and soon, five hundred yards across the marsh from us, came the sound of chopping as they readied a blind. Chad was worried.

"No open water there, but that's the place where the mallards come in here from the St. Croix River. Those muzzlers are right in front of a low pass through the hills. Them mallards come through there like you opened a door for 'em."

There was at least an hour's wait to shooting time. The two old hands puttered with the blind. They rigged crotched sticks to keep their shotgun breeches away from the dribbling sand of the blind's wall. They made comfortable seats for themselves, and finally, as was their right by seniority, they wrapped the old horse blanket about their knees, with the lantern beneath, and toasted their shins in stinking comfort.

Long before there was any real light, ducks returned to our open water, and the ODHA, waiting nervously, sipped coffee and made a career out of not clinking the aluminum cups. In that blind with Mister President it was almost worth a man's life to kick a shellbox accidentally in the dark.

Chad briefed us: "When the time comes, don't nobody miss on them first ones, 'cause our friends over there are situated to scare out incomers. That is, in case they get a shot. Praise be, neither one of them are cloudbusters."

As the zero hour approached Mister President produced his gold watch and chain, and the two of them followed the snail's pace of the minute hand.

"Good idea not to jump the gun," said Chad. "No use to break the law."

To which Mister President added: "Might be a game warden hanging around, too."

"Now!"

As Mister President gave the word Chad kicked his shellbox and stood up. The air was full of flailing wings. I missed one, got it with the second barrel and heard three calculated shots from Mister President's automatic. I also heard Chad's cussing. He had forgotten to load his cornsheller. The air was a bright cerulean blue until his city conscience smote them and he said remorsefully, "Wash me and I shall be whiter than snow."

With daylight the wind shifted from the northwest to northeast and the snow began again, from Lake Superior this time. That kind of snow at that season is not to be trifled with, for northeasters can blow for three days and fetch mighty drifts. I picked up the drake mallard I had downed and the three birds Mister President had collected in his methodical way. The two old hands agreed that none of the mallards were locals, but "Redlegs down from Canada – feel the heft of that one!"

There was a long wait after that first burst of shooting. Obviously there were not many ducks left in the country. The original ODHA comforted themselves with hot coffee and thick sandwiches. From time to time one of them ascended the little knob at our rear to look across the snowy marsh and observe operations over there.

Chad came back from a reconnaissance and exclaimed, "She's workin', glory be."

The words were hardly out of his mouth when five mallards materialized out of the smother, circled the open water and cupped wings to drop in. As they zoomed in Mister President and Chad picked off a drake apiece, and when the wind had blown them to the edge of the ice I picked them up.

"You got him broke pretty well," Chad observed.

"Fair, just fair," grunted Mister President, squinting through the snow. "He's steady to wing and shot, but a mite nervous on in-comers. Needs more field work."

Shortly before noon I climbed the hill myself for a look across the marsh. Through the snow over the high flaggers I could make out the dark green blob that was the jack-pine blind of the butcher and piano tuner. We had not heard a shot from the place. As I watched six mallards, mere specks at first, approached the marsh from the direction of the St. Croix River. They were coming through the low hill pass just as Chad had said they would. Normally they would have flown almost directly over the distant blind.

Some distance from the blind I saw them flare and climb, then swing wide around the edge of the marsh and sail straight into our open hole. From my vantage point I saw the two old hands rise and fire, and three ducks fell.

Mister President called up to me: "Pick up that one that dropped in the scrub, will yuh?"

"We'd better keep careful count," Chad suggested. In a few minutes he dropped two more that tried to sneak into the water hole.

"I'm through," he announced. He acknowledged his limit with a thankful verse: "Thou hast turned for me my mourning into dancing."

The afternoon moved along. The snow increased, and when limits were had all around we finished the last of the soup, washed it down with the now lukewarm coffee and picked up. It was high time we were moving. A good six inches of snow was on the ground. There were steep, slippery hills between us and the main road.

Back at the car, we turned the behemoth around. Parked just to the rear of us was the conveyance of the piano tuner and the butcher. It was a modern job with the low-slung build of a dachshund, but in maneuvering out of the place Mister President's locomotive-like contraption broke out a good trail.

Mister President and Chad were jubilant as the big car was tooled carefully over the crooked road to Norm's, where we picked up gear left behind in the unlighted cabin hours before and said goodby to Norm – "until the smallmouth take a notion to hit in the St. Croix."

Homeward bound. Chad's best Sunday *basso profundo* broke into a sincere rendition of an old hymn which emphasizes that "He will carry you through," and Mister President joined him with a happy, off-key baritone. We halted at the curb in front of Chad's house, and he emerged from the car laden with mallards and gear and smelling of horse blanket and kerosene.

"We sure fooled 'em," said Mister President.

"Thou preparest a table for me in the presence of mine enemies," Chad intoned, and went up his walk to the door.

At Mister President's back door I helped him with the unloading. What, I demanded, was the thing Chad had removed from Gus Blomberg's front yard?

"Well, sir," said Mister President. "It was a device calculated to do the undoable and solve the unsolvable. I couldn't have done better myself."

He sat down on a shellbox on his back steps the better to laugh at his partner's cunning.

"You know," he said, "When he stuck that thing out there just in the right place, he came back to the blind and told me, 'Mine enemies are lively and they are strong'."

"What was it?" I insisted. "All I know is there was something out there that made those mallards flare."

Hizzoner picked up the shellbox, his hand on the door knob, and said, "It was Gus Blomberg's scarecrow, and I'm surprised you haven't figured it out."

"All I could guess was that it was something made of tin cans. I heard 'em rattle."

"Gus Blomberg," said Mister President, "always drapes tin cans on his scarecrows soste they'll rattle in the wind. Good night to you, sir – and don't forget to come over tomorrow night and help me pick these ducks."

❧

– Paul Birling

August Derleth was born February 24, 1909 in Sauk City, Wisconsin, where he spent his life as an author, publisher, editor, naturalist, journalist, poet and environmentalist. He died unexpectedly on July 4, 1971 at the age of 61. He is still known as Wisconsin's most prolific writer, having authored over 150 books, and having written more about the history of Wisconsin and the Wisconsin River than anyone else.

The complexity of his nature and his tremendously creative output combined to produce a most unusual man. His contribution to American literature is a source of ongoing speculation and amazement as new generations of readers discover his work. Interest in him and his writing continues to grow, which is evident in his 350-member, worldwide fan club, the August Derleth Society.

Derleth was an environmentalist before it was popular, and his writings detail his observations about plants and animals. He worried that man would destroy himself, and charted the evidence in his many journals. His works include novels of almost every genre: nature, romance, history, poetry, journals, mystery, boys' books and science fiction. And always, he wrote about the people in his small town, revealing emotions every reader can identify with as universal to mankind.

Derleth's reputation as an outdoorsman is secondary only to his respect for and love of nature. From the first pasque flower of spring to the last blizzard of winter, Derleth recorded his love affair with life and nature. His insight into our world continues to offer readers an understanding unique in its limitless scope.

Walden West

by
August Derleth

The Spring Slough was the magnet which drew me afternoons and evenings in the spring, and early in the morning hours of many summer days. It was a long body of water, ranging in depth from a few inches to eight feet, begun with a large, relatively shallow lake or pond north of the trestle, carrying through a narrower neck to a wider portion which stretched away between tree-girt banks almost to the brook in the south. Blue flags lined its shores, with cattails, Joe-Pye weed, buttonball bushes, osiers, willows, soft maples, birches, elms; yellow pond lilies grew on its surface, and in its shallows arrowleaf flourished, and at all times, in hot weather, great masses of sphagnum dotted its water. Like all the other sloughs along the Wisconsin, it was spring fed, though, before the level of the Wisconsin fell as a result of watershed controls at its headwaters, the slough was refreshed by a torrent of water from the swollen river every April and June.

The Spring Slough teemed with wildlife. I used to sit on the trestle absorbed in the movement of muskrats, which went about their lives up and down the slough, foraging, mating, fighting; in the less obtrusive lives of bluewinged teal and mallards and wood ducks and their fledglings learning to swim and take care of themselves; in the circumspect caution of beavers, come from the colony house to cross the slough to where young willows and poplar growth offered them food, watching them climb out on the banks, cut a sapling, section it, and gnaw away the bark. Painted turtles occupied the logs which were always to be found in the slough, splashing off as I came along, climbing back out of the water after making sure that I meant them no harm. And occasionally otters invaded the slough, coming up from the brook, spending their infectious joy in diving and playing and hunting the slough for an hour before returning the way they had come, their joyous cries falling away behind them.

The water was never still. Muskrats and turtles broke it; now and then a brown water snake slithered by; flies danced over its surface; sunfish rose, and great northerns came to surface and swirled away; the summer cricket frogs climbed out on the lilypads and ballooned their throats in song, as in the spring months the hylidae crowded the shallows along the shore and filled the day and night alike with their primal music. On rare occasions a mink or weasel made its way along the shores, in silent, relentless hunting.

Phoebes and pewees nested in the vicinity; warblers –
particularly, in season, prothonotaries and blackburnians – and all
summer long, redstarts, myrtle and other nesting warblers fed upon
the flies and mosquitoes and gnats which were always present above
the water. Redwings sang out of the Upper Meadow, which spread
away east of the slough and the railroad tracks to the Mazomanie
road and, beyond it, the low hills where the moraine tapered off
from the north before coming up against the more formidable
Wisconsin Heights in the southeast, the setting of the only near
battle of the Black Hawk War. Crows always cried from all horizons,
and very often majestic hawks – redtails, red-shoulders, ospreys –
soared, screaming, out of the woods and high above the slough and
the meadows and the hills, up against the wind, into the air
currents, there to float in lonely serenity, sometimes with their
mates to engage in an inspiring show of love play, high, high, over,
almost invisible, commanding all the woods and the river bottoms
and the hills, while great blue herons came gliding into the slough
to stand motionless in the sun-dappled shallows fishing. Now and
then harriers quartered the meadow for the mice which were in the
deep grasses by the thousands, adding their small rustlings to the
symphony of nature's voices always to be heard in this place
throughout the green seasons.

As the afternoon waned and the long shadows crossed the
slough, some voices were stilled, and others rose – mourning doves,
cardinals, field sparrows, and, as darkness came on, the nostalgic
song of the whippoorwills, and, above all, the crying of the frogs –
the peepers in a great choir out of the Upper Meadow, the cricket
frogs from nearer the slough, the pond frogs conversing across the
water, the woods frogs uttering their hoarse croaking out of the tree-
grown bottomland to the west – all pulsing and throbbing as in the
very rhythm of earth itself. I never tired of listening to the frogs'
primal music, which seemed to me to convey implicitly a continuity
that carried back to the beginning of time and would carry on to its

end. This was true, too, of the hot stridulation of cicadas on summer days. Sometimes, when I stayed late of April and May nights, the east banks of the slough were invaded by boys from the village, come down to fish for bullheads. They sat just south of the trestle, or up along the shore of the pond, near a bonfire, which made its orange glow warmly in the darkness; very often I joined them for a little while, taking a pole, or sitting at the fire making the kind of small talk which is essential to village life – of weather, local politics, the trivial events which seem so important in the life of such a social unit as a small town – come inside, as it were, for a little while, and returning again to the cosmos outside where the sustaining voices were not the hum of life in Sac Prairie but the voices of the winds, the talking leaves, the siren music of interplanetary spaces.

I used to sit on the Spring Slough Trestle to read and write and dream, spending time as wisely as I knew, watching the years pass, at first slowly, and then with increasing swiftness, and never counted a moment there ill spent.

❖

Nothing more arresting comes out of the woods of a summer night than the song of the pewee. Be it in two notes or three, or perhaps one long drawn-out keening note, the song's nostalgia makes its instant appeal to ear and heart. It comes drifting out of the woods darkening with dusk and twilight, a voice belonging to that world of half dark, though it is no less to be heard at mid-day, when it is but one among a score of others. It arrests, it challenges, it seduces with its invitation to anyone outside that perimeter of darkness, drawing him in, in spirit, certainly, if the flesh but stand to pay its tribute to that invisible singer.

The song of the pewee seems to stand for all that is unknown about a woods. Why this should be so, I do not know, but I understand that one comes to listen for the pewee's voice year after year, as I do. Anyone heeding that invitation to come into the darkening woods would seldom see its source, for the woods at night is a place in which to come face to face with one's self, to acknowledge the mote-like insignificance of man in this cosmos. I think of the pewee sometimes as the essential voice of the woods, though the song is often little more than a breath, a whisper, a small keening which drifts out upon the evening air like a melody from time gone by, yet it commands the ear, it challenges the heart, it demands awareness that here in these notes the woods speaks to every listening ear.

Too, it is the summer's one unfailing voice, raised in every kind of weather, dry or hot, wet, humid or windy, cloying or cool, the one unwavering voice which speaks for the depths of the woods in which by night there are so many fugitive movements and sounds, rustlings, snapping twigs, strange muted voices, which symbolize that vast, intimate life being lived without cognizance almost side by side with the humming mills of the human beings who are still so far from any integration with the land. In its own way, this dulcet song is as beguiling as any aspect of the woods at night, and as unknown; dusk and darkness are its proper conditions; the enclosing woods its most fitting milieu. It speaks for the woods, it speaks for all the wild earth, asking over and over for man to come in, to come back to that primitive intimacy with the earth and the sky, with brooks and trees and hills and all mankind's wild brothers.

Pe-wee, pe-wee, it says, *Pe-a-wee* . . .

Come in, come in, it says. Be not afraid . . .

– making its invitation throughout dusk and darkness, speaking for the forever mysterious woods, where the very trees in their windy susurration seem to hush and respire, respire and hush with the pulse of unknown night and the rhythm of the planet on its way through eternity.

✤

The essence of autumn is in the soft October evenings, mellow and hazed with pungent smoke, deriving, old-timers say, from cranberry marshes or forests burning somewhere up north – never from any certain source, evenings lit with leaf fires here and there, and echoing with the honking of geese flying south, following the great bend of the Wisconsin at Sac Prairie and confused by the diffused glow of the lights from the village, circling blindly overhead, hour after hour, deep into night. Something is in such evenings that touches upon man's racial experience, that reaches far back into the ancestry of mankind and forges a link to today and tomorrow.

Smoke and haze, pungence and musk, darkness and bonfire glow – and from overhead the troubled crying of the geese, briefly lost – the geese which are no small part of the night's intimacy or of that dark mystery which carries the very exhalation of the autumn earth to the sensitive and sentient among men – all are symbolic of flight from the moment, the escape from self which seems to everyone sometimes so necessary, so desirable. Perhaps these migrant birds represent the passage of man himself from birth to death, the continuity of which every man is in his own way aware throughout his existence. Bird and man, each in his cycle, obeys his own dark laws.

✤

There are afternoons in late autumn or early winter, during that recessive period of the year when the sun is low in the southern sky, when a special kind of light lies on the face of the familiar marshes. Snow has not yet fallen, or has thawed and gone, the land is brown, dun-colored, grey, with every vestige of the vernal seasons varnished save only for the tight buds on the maples. But in this very drabness – relieved only by osiers' red, the mustard of willows, and the many-colored lichens, and here and there in a sheltered nook, a sturdy green blade – which maintains wherever the eye courses, the sunlight lingers; it falls at an angle which invests every blade and seed-head with a life it has at no other time, for sunlight gleams from the blades of the dry rushes and the grasses, it shines off the twigs and limbs of willows and osiers, it glows supernally from the seed-heads of goldenrod, wild clematis, milkweed and dogbane, the dying cattails and the thistles, and off the climbing false buckwheat seedpods it sheds a mellow tan effulgence, so that for a few hours of every afternoon, warm or cold, the meadows and the marshes seem endowed with a special kind of sentience in the soft sienna haze which holds to everything as were it the tangibility of sunlight itself. And through the middle of it the rails of the roadbed reflect the sun more brightly than anything else, leading away in the direction of the sun itself, through the meadows, past the ponds, sloughs, grassy regions and rush-grown hummocks, past brook and leaning maple, past willow grove and silky cornel, as if to mark the only possible direction through this unreality which cloaks the familiar scenes of spring and summer with an iridescence which holds within it not alone the certainty of winter, but also the assurance of spring once more.

❖

If there is one winter voice informed with wildness, it is the crow's. Temperature is a matter of moment to him; he sends his challenge over the landscape whenever and wherever he pleases, but in winter he is more in evidence than in other seasons, not alone because his is one of the few voices to be heard in and about Sac Prairie, but because he extends his range in the season of snow and ice, deserting the hills and marshes adjacent to the Wisconsin to fly out over the prairie and the fields beyond, passing over into the company of his fellows, and returning before dark to his roost, secure in his mastery of the heavens.

Being the epitome of wildness, he is canny as well as arrogant, and in every attribute he has, his essential independence of man stands out. Whereas sparrows, robins, starlings, even nighthawks, and a host of lesser birds do not trouble themselves about and often elect the company of mankind, the crow shuns it, mocks it, derides and keeps his distance from even a lone walker in the woods at any season. But winter is peculiarly the crow's season; however more difficult may be his foraging, he seems in this season to come into his own, hurling his challenge from every corner of the grey winter sky, constantly about in all manner of weather.

He is good company, paradoxically better at a distance, for nearby his cries are harsh, forbidding, while at a diminishing range toward the horizon his calls are mellowed by distance and the quality of the air – its dryness of humidity; they are crisp or liquid, with an almost musical quality seldom heard at close quarters. One never doubts, hearing him, that he is the woods' master, the admiral of the snowy wastes where he and his companions command the heavens virtually alone, dark on the grey or somber blue sky, dark on the white landscape below.

In the sound of his caw is the proof of his wildness. Here clearly is the voice of one who has resisted all the blandishments of civilization, who has defied the best efforts of man to tame or slay him. It is curious to reflect that the crow's voice should comfort a man in his solitude, however much the crow's rascality be known; yet it is so. It is as if this proof of the essential wildness of this black scavenger were an immutable assurance of the persistence of the wildness, of the continuity of life itself, for there is never any dearth of crows – they survive every season, they escape the most dedicated hunter, they return as inevitably as the seasons themselves.

⁜

No winter is ever so long or so bitter but that, by mid-March, the ear is attuned to that first harsh *zeep* which announces the return of the woodcock and is but a prelude to the vaulting ecstasy of the bird's aerial dance. Sometimes the bird arrives as early as the fourteenth of March; sometimes not for two weeks later; but whenever that first nasal *zeep* rises out of the chilly twilight, whenever that dark body first hurtles aloft in its wonderfully stirring dance against the evening heavens, the silence and the darkness of the winter nights are done for another year. But not until then – for the early killdeer ceases to call with the setting sun, and so, too, do the redwings and the bluebirds and the song sparrows which might have preceded the woodcocks' return. Only the woodcocks cry and dance for some hours into the night, beginning not long after sundown.

In this avian ecstasy, there is inherent an experience which enriches all who behold it, something primal, something which went on before the arrival on the scene of man and his works, something which may last beyond man. I never tired of watching the aerial dance of the woodcocks, and on several occasions I managed, by dint of perseverance, to make my way to the place from which the bird had risen – once he was safely aloft – for the woodcock habitually returns to approximately the same spot from which it rises. On one evening, I sat on a stump while this long-billed songster stood within reach, less than two feet away, making his harsh calls, tipping his body awkwardly with each cry, and vaulting suddenly into the heavens, to circle with the wind winnowing in his wings, chirping excitedly in his mating dance.

I learned in this manner that approximately five seconds elapsed between the end of the descent after a flight aloft, and the beginning of the next round of calls, a period of time which seldom varied unless the bird were disturbed, though the number of calls before the dance took place again varied considerably. Watching that awkward body while the bird called made that ecstatic flight seem all the more impressive with an impressiveness and a primal beauty which belong to this rite of spring as to no other.

The first promise of the spring evening, after the long, still winter nights, lies in the rapture of the woodcocks, in which instantly all the tribulations of the frozen season are dimmed and lost.

❧

— *Sandy Klein Stevens*

If you enjoyed

Harvest Moon:

A Wisconsin Outdoor Anthology

Call our toll-free number

800/336-3091

or write to

Lost River Press, Inc.

P.O. Box 1381

Woodruff, WI 54568

to find out more about our other titles concerning nature and the outdoor experience.

We welcome your questions and comments about our products, and urge you to let us know how we might better serve you.